LOST IN

APPALACHIA

LOST IN

APPALACHIA

Hiding our Resources in Small-Town America

Continuing the Dancing Deer Series with Book 4

Ron Lambert

Copyright © 2012 by Ron Lambert

Published in the United States by:

Printers Guild Publishing House, llc

425 Spring Street, Suite 101
Columbus, Texas 78934-2461
(979) 732-2962   Fax (979) 733-0015
www.printersguildpublshing.com

Library of Congress Control Number: 2013914819

ISBN 978-0-9855083-5-7

Lost in Appalanchia is a work of Fiction

Except for some historical personages the names, characters, and incidents of the story are used fictitiously and do not represent any actual person or event.

Some of the towns, cities, or geographic localities are real. An interested reader might be able to find Lee Mountain, the Buffalo River, the Illinois Bayou, the Big Piney, Moccasin Gap, or even Little Creek's water crossing. Eudy's might be harder.

The author grew up in a small rural community and saw wonder in all living things. He wrote this story using the hazy remembrances of a child's fertile imagination and sheer luck.

Trademarks

Cover

Picture from Shutterstock.com

CONTENTS

CHAPTER 1—ADELLE
November, 1925

Adelle stepped out of her comfort zone. She was always the conservative one, never drawing attention to herself. She lived a quiet life as the only child of a part-time school teacher and a frail, loving mother. Before going away to college, Adelle had never traveled outside Pittsburgh. She'd read books—was a regular at the library—and dreamed of far away places, exotic places. But Adelle had been home-schooled and, outside of her books, had a myopic view of life.

When she started college, it took every penny her father could raise to pay her first semester's tuition. Then someone from the state board of education said if Adelle taught in her home state after graduation, the Commonwealth of Pennsylvania would pay her remaining tuition through graduation.

Three years later, at twenty-two, Adelle lost her father to tuberculosis and her mother to a broken heart. Her father's illness was short-lived. He'd probably been suffering for a long time but kept it to himself. He'd always had a cough and no one thought anything about it, until one day Adelle's mother found blood on his handkerchief. He died within the month, and her mother became bedridden.

Between Adelle's parents he'd been the tough one. Adelle's father had taken care of his wife. The woman suffered through the whooping cough, shingles, stomach problems, breathing disorders, and a cold with each change of the season. Adelle's father had learned to cook, to clean house, and to minister to his wife's needs. When he died, no one was there to take his place. Adelle was in a small women's college a hundred miles away, and Adelle's grandfather had not been in their home during the last fifteen years.

Adelle sent her grandfather a telegram saying her father had died and her mother was extremely ill. Adelle couldn't cope. It had been hard for her and her mother to actually acknowledge Adelle's father was gone. The 1940's was not his time. Pennsylvania was not his place. Adelle's father was a man out of sync.

9

After a week of telling each other everything would be all right, Adelle and her mother thought it best if Adelle continued her education. She was beginning her senior year. Adelle later decided she should have stayed with her mother.

One day, not many months later, the postman delivered a letter. Her mother was sick. It was either the shaky hand, the tear-stained smudges, or the nonchalant way her mother suggested Adelle come home a weekend very soon that told Adelle. She put the letter in her pocket, gathered her things, and left that same afternoon. Her classes would still be there when she returned. Adelle raced home to find her mother barely conscious. A neighboring nurse prodded and hovered, following the doctor's instructions.

Adelle's mother had always been frail. When her life's companion died, he took away her will to live. She just curled up and withered.

Adelle remembered her grandfather as a tyrant. He yelled at her mother and ranted at her father's inability to provide. She also remembered her parents' proud refusal of her grandfather's offer to help. They were now alone, the three of them—soon to be two.

Torguson Ripley was nearing seventy when he arrived. Hale and hearty, he never understood the sickly nature of his only child. When she entered the world, she was turned the wrong way and entangled with the umbilical cord. The labor was long and painful. Torguson's wife lost so much blood, she died soon after giving the final push. She held her baby one time before the light dimmed in her eyes.

Torguson had to raise his daughter with help from his spinster sister. A star baseball player he spent long periods on the road. His sister did the best she could, but the child caught everything under the sun. His sister plied her niece with homespun remedies routinely passed from mother to daughter, but nothing helped.

One day, many years later when his daughter was in high school, Torguson received a note from the girl's teacher saying his daughter had missed so much school she was having difficulty keeping up. The teacher suggested he hire a tutor. His daughter fell in love with the tutor.

Adelle met her grandfather at the train station, and he immediately took charge. She couldn't handle the details, but he could and he did. Adelle's grandfather arrived the day before her mother died. The doctors said they were losing her, and the old man sat beside his daughter's placid body, held her thin waxy hand in both of his, and cried. Adelle was in and out of the bedroom, but her grandfather never left her mother's presence. He sat beside the bed in a chair facing the door and talked to Adelle's mother all night. Adelle knew her mother was in a coma and probably couldn't hear what he said, but whatever he said was important to him. Adelle put her ear to the door, but she could only make out a single word every so often. When she opened the door and entered, her grandfather stopped talking. He dabbed his eyes with a cotton handkerchief, and when she left, he started in again.

Adelle thought her grandfather grieved for the years he'd been away. She knew he desperately tried to talk her mother out of marrying the young man "with nothing but the change in his pockets," but her mother was determined. It became a test of wills. For the first time in her life, Adelle's mother stood up to Adelle's grandfather for her independence and for the love of her life. The couple soon married and began testing the time-honored proverb that "you can't live on love alone." They gave it their best shot. Adelle's father, the tutor, was a visionary radical without a foot in the real world. He and her mother loved each other deeply but had to live a pauper's lifestyle.

When Adelle's aunt died, Adelle and her mother were her grandfather's only kin. After years of yelling, they became distant through lack of contact. Then, similar to a racehorse who is cast off when his legs won't let him run and the drugs are unable to make him competitive, her grandfather left the game he loved and wandered west looking without knowing for what.

Torguson stopped for a while in Hot Springs, Arkansas, where the mineral waters gushed hot from underground springs. They allowed him to deal with his bum knees and stiff joints. The hotter the water, the better he felt. Then one day as he traveled in the northern part of the state, Adelle's grandfather heard of a farm with its own thermal mineral spring. It lay on the outskirts of a little town known as Dancing Deer.

Torguson pestered the owner until the man threw up his hands, pocketed the proffered funds, and headed to California.

Torguson arranged for the funeral. He buried his daughter, not far from his wife, on a small knoll. The tutor was moved from the pauper's section to lay beside his wife, Torguson's daughter. A large granite tombstone was placed over both graves. Torguson sat on a concrete bench beside the three graves and listened to whispering oaks lament their loss, their limbs rustled in the breeze. From the small knoll he could see a winding river snaking through brown fields and finally disappearing into the mist.

Torguson wondered how he could have handled things differently. Too much pride, too much of the high-and-mighty, too much sanctimonious authority, too much stupidity. Why does clear vision come through watery eyes?

Torguson's daughter had few possessions: her house belonged to someone else; her clothes were frayed, repair made on repair; and her household furnishings and kitchen items had been donated from neighbors. Adelle kept a few items for sentimental reasons, and everything else she either gave to charity or cast away.

Torguson convinced Adelle to go back to college. He told her she could come to Dancing Deer after she graduated. He then paid Adelle's back tuition, relieving her of the teaching obligation, and went home to prepare for his granddaughter's arrival.

Torguson spent the next six months sprucing up his farm. He had a barrel cooper construct a gigantic, water-tight half-barrel of seasoned oak for the hot mineral water. The half-barrel was ten feet in diameter and included built-in benches. It was placed behind the house in the middle of a flower bed. A plumber installed a pump at the spring and buried pipe all the way to his house ending with a spigot in the middle of the barrel. A drain let the mineral-rich water seep through thick mulch to keep his flowers lush and green. He could smell the roses and lounge with or without clothing. But, Torguson would soon have to start acting more dignified. No longer would sitting in a rocky hole be appropriate. And when he lounged in his new barrel he would need to be wearing swimming trunks.

Adelle arrived in the early Spring. He'd already hired a housekeeper and a cook. Adelle thought he had plenty of money. She was told, in his playing days, Ty Cobb had convinced him to invest in a small Georgia company called Coca Cola. Her grandfather now lived off that investment. Of course, Ty Cobb investing considerable more money than Adelle's grandfather, became the wealthiest ballplayer there had ever been.

After Adelle had been there a couple of months, she and her grandfather, one cool evening, sat soaking in the barrel.

"Honey, what's your wildest dream?"

Adelle thought of being with a man. Would she ever get married? Would a suitor ever break down the door to whisk her away? Would she ever be kissed . . . her hand held? She remembered the stories told about her mother announcing her love for the tutor and said, "I'd like to travel."

CHAPTER 2—APPALACHIA
September 1945

Chester maneuvered his boat down the line. He had a two-hundred-foot trout line carrying four thousand hooks. He didn't bait the hooks. Weighted and staggered in height from one to six feet, he tied their leads every half-inch on the main line. Chester caught his prey when an unlucky creature swam too close and became entangled in the mass of hooks.

Today, Chester's haul included a man, barely alive. Chester hauled him aboard and paddled back to his home on the banks of an Oogala River tributary.

In a strong voice, Chester boomed, "Demas, get out here and help me."

Demas, Chester's half-witted son, had been cutting firewood. Hearing his name, he stuck the ax, and headed to where his dad kept the john-boat.

"What'd you catch, Daddy? A big 'ole river cat?"

"Naw, help me get him to the house. I caught a drifter this time."

"Wow, he's still alive. I hear him breathing. You catch him on the line?"

"Yeah, took an hour to get him untangled. He had one leg stretched on top of a log. Must've been there for hours."

Chester and Demas carried the man inside the house. No one wanted to give up a bed, so Charley, Demas' older sister, made a pallet in a corner of the front room beside the fire. She used a frayed towel to dry the man as best she could. Demas then removed the man's long shirt that extended to his knees and replaced his dirty, torn underwear with a pair of ragged but clean underwear from his dad's room.

Demas said, "Is he hurt?"

Chester sat at the table. "'Course he's hurt. See that crusted-over wound on the back of his head? Good thing he was able to keep it outta the water, otherwise, the catfish would've eaten him like bait."

Charley moved the man's arms and feet. "I don't think he's got any broken bones."

"Ow."

"Maybe a broken rib or two." Charley propped up the man's head with the wadded towel. "Mister, you want something to eat?"

"What ya got, Charley?" Chester thought he might like something as well.

"Just what's left from breakfast. I ain't started lunch yet." Charley looked back at the man. His eyes were half open. "You got a name? You want something to eat?"

The man nodded.

Charley left and came back in a moment with a biscuit and two pieces of cold sausage. The man reached for the biscuit, grimaced, and let his hand fall to the floor.

"Yep, he's got a broken rib. You better wrap something real tight around his chest."

"Here, mister." Charley fed him the biscuit and two pieces of sausage then left, returning with a clean rag. She wrapped it tight around his chest, then ripped and tied the ends together. After eating, the man fell asleep as orange and yellow tongues licked the rocks of the fireplace.

That night, the man started shaking. Charley felt his forehead and announced he'd caught the fever. He eventually lost consciousness, then started mumbling incoherently. Chester and his family thought the man would die before morning, but when the dawn broke his condition was still the same. They thought he might make it another day, but probably would be gone by the end of the week.

The fever lasted three days. Charley fed him and cleaned his mess. By the fourth day, he was sitting up.

"Mister, you feeling better?"

The man nodded.

"You want something to eat?"

He nodded again.

Charley brought over a plate with a slice of ham, cornbread, and pinto beans. "I'll cut the ham."

The man nodded.

"You got a name? We got to start calling you something other than mister."

The man shook his head.

"You ain't got a name?"

"Don't know what it is."

"You running from somebody?"

"Don't know."

"Well, I'm going to start calling you Pierre."

"Let's go with some other name."

"Okay, you like Tom?"

"Yeah, Tom's all right."

"Where you from, Tom? How'd you get in the river?"

"Don't know."

Charley handed Tom the plate of food. While he ate, she picked up a book and sat down. "You know how to read?"

Tom looked at the book. It was a dictionary. He reached for it, opened it up, squinted at the blurred words, and said, "Yeah, I can read."

"Would you teach me?"

"Sure, but you'll need a book."

"What about this one?"

"No, this one won't work. What's your name?"

"Charley."

"Charley, you need a novel."

"A novel? Where am I gonna find a novel?"

"Is there a town close by?"

"Naw, but the Pike brothers will be coming soon. I'll ask them. They bring us what we can't grow or catch and trade for pelts and sides of venison. They'll be by next week. I'll ask them to bring a novel."

"How do they get here?"

"Come down the river on a barge."

"Aren't there any roads?"

"Naw, just the river."

"And no towns?"

"Yeah, we got towns. Danville's two days down the river and Brewster is three days up. Brewster's closer but takes longer going upstream."

"There any schools?"

"No, Pa can read though. He lived in Brewster when he was a kid. Momma lived in Danville. They settled here between the two towns."

"What happened to your mother?"

"Got bit by a cottonmouth. Her leg swelled up, turned purple, then yellow, and burst open."

"She step on it?"

"No, it crawled in bed with her looking for a mouse or something and bit her leg when she rolled over on top of it."

"Damn."

"Yeah, Pa was gone to Brewster on a drunk and me and Demas were just toddlers. When Pa got back she was dead."

"Well, Charley, you get me a novel from the Pike brothers—a Nancy Drew mystery or a Hardy Boys adventure—and some paper and a pencil, and I'll teach you how to read and write."

CHAPTER 3—LYSISTRATA
Dancing Deer

"Hello, you Mrs. Springer?"

"Yes, I am."

"I've got a delivery for you, a hundred pounds of peas. I've got orders to deliver a hundred pounds of peas to you each week for five weeks. Where do you want me to put them?"

"A hundred pounds of peas? You must be mistaken. I didn't order any peas."

"Yes, ma'am, it says on my order, these are your husband's winnings. I'm to pick them up shelled and canned next week when I deliver your next batch. I'll unload them here unless you want me to carry them into your kitchen."

"No—now, wait a minute—you say they're my husband's winnings, but I've got to give them back after I've shelled and canned them?"

"Yes, ma'am."

"You stay right here while I go call my husband. I think someone's made a dreadful mistake."

"That's the same thing Mrs. Abernathy said when I delivered her the corn."

"Suzanne Abernathy's shucking corn?"

"Yes, ma'am. I delivered a hundred pounds of corn to her earlier this morning."

"And she's going to can it and give it back to you?"

"Yes, ma'am. She's got five hundred pounds coming—same as you."

"That's preposterous. Suzanne only cans when she's entered a competition. No one ever gets to open her canned goods. And, besides that, she gets a manicure every week. There's no way she's gonna shuck corn. You stay here. I'll be right back."

Clarice Springer was married to Robert Springer, sometimes referred to as Mayor Bob. He'd bet the New York Hotshots would beat the Men from Dancing Deer, known by the city council as the Peckerwoods, in a game of baseball. He lost, and now he, his wife, and their two young daughters would have to shell five hundred pounds of peas. Bob was in a deep pile of dung.

"Bob, darling, can you tell me about a bet you made involving peas?"

"Uh . . . baby, I meant to tell you about that, but I can't talk right now. I've got somebody in my office."

In a sugary voice Clarice said, "Bob, darling, you get your sweet little ass . . ." Her voice raised to a low roar, "home in fifteen minutes or there won't be any need for you to come home." She slammed down the phone.

Back on the front porch, she found five large boxes of peas stacked next to her swing.

"Ma'am, you going to be shelling on the swing? I can carry them inside if you want."

"No, that'll be all right. Does your order say who sent them?"

"No, ma'am, but the finished product will be going to the food pantry. I think Mrs. Millhouse has been slated to run it Mondays, Wednesdays, and Fridays till noon."

"Mona Millhouse?"

"Yes, ma'am. She starts the first week in November and works through Christmas. Someone else will take over then."

"I'm sure there's a rational explanation for all this, and as soon as my husband gets home, I'll find out what it is. You got more deliveries to make?"

"No, ma'am."

Clarice spun around on her heels and slammed the screen door in the delivery boy's face.

"H'mm, pretty much the same as Mrs. Abernathy."

Clarice went into the house and called Suzanne. She wanted answers and she wanted them now. "Suzanne? This is Clarice. Do you know anything about a bet our husbands have made?"

"No, but when Rube gets home, I'm going to find out. My kitchen's full of corn. A delivery boy said I should get to shucking and canning as he'll be bringing me another delivery next week."

"Suzanne, I'm going to call Mona. Maybe she knows. I'll get back to you when I've got the details."

Clarice then dialed Mona Millhouse. "Hello, Mona? This is Clarice. Do you know anything about a bet our husbands have made?"

"No. Jerry hasn't said anything to me about any bets."

"Then you don't know you're scheduled to man a food pantry starting the first week in November?"

"No, certainly not. Where'd you hear such a thing?"

"I'll get back to you when I've got more information."

Mayor Bob pulled up, jumped out of his car, and ran to the house. He saw the boxes of peas by the swing as he slid to the screen door.

"Baby, I can explain."

"Sit down, Robert. You better make this good."

"Me and the other members of the City Council thought we'd finally bested Bill. We had him dead to rights, then he made his wife the manager of the Peckerwoods. Who in their wildest dreams could've known she was a professional? And damn if she didn't beat the Hotshots. Now we got to feed the poor this winter, and our family's job is to shell a few peas."

"You might have to, but you can rot in hell before you'll persuade me and the girls to help."

"Oh, baby. That was part of the written agreement. I sell insurance. How many policies do you think will get shifted to the competition if the town learns I bet against the Peckerwoods? You and the girls have to help or Bill goes straight to the paper. And you're smart enough to figure out that if I have a down turn in my business you'll have to get a job or we'll lose the house.

"You show us how to shell those peas and me and the girls will help you get it done."

Clarice stood before the gathered women. "Is everyone here fully aware of the wagers our husbands have made?"

The attending women started talking among themselves. "It was an outrage."

"It was unthinkable."

"They ought to be shot."

"What were they thinking?"

"Please, ladies, we have to think of an appropriate response. We can't let this go without retaliating in some meaningful way. Does anyone have an idea? The chair recognizes Suzanne."

"I think we ought to let the men muddle their way through this. I, for one, am fed up with canning day after day. Sure, Rube helps. He's even got our son washing the jars, but the majority of the work has been heaped on my shoulders. I'm thinking of pulling up a chair and directing their work while I read a book."

"At least you don't have to climb a ladder with a bucket of paint. My John says he's afraid of heights. He's got the children painting everything up to the tops of their heads, while he paints from there to the top of his, and then he expects me to climb a ladder and get the entire second story. Yesterday I poured a bucket of paint on his head. He laughed and said, 'Honey, we got to get this one painted and on to the next. It's no time to play.' My John says each painting family has to finish a building every two weeks to meet the wager's deadline."

"Stone had to show us how to use a spinning, rotisserie-looking thing and a router. We're making toys. I got one boy making tops and yo-yos and another building dollhouses. My daughter is trying to braid thread for throwing the tops and yo-yos. At eight, she's having a helluva time getting her fingers working properly and keeping her eyes off the pretty doll-houses."

"What're you doing, Marge?"

"I'm cutting and sewing doll clothes."

"Okay, ladies, I agree we're being taken to the cleaners, but what I want to know is if there is something we can do to make the men pay. I do believe we have to help our husbands get their bets paid so their names stay out of the paper. Also, I want to be able to sit in church and not hear hushed whispers behind my back. But the men have to pay." Clarice looked around the room. "The chair recognizes Ophelia Obadiah."

"I once attended a Greek play where the women were so upset with their husbands' aggressive behavior, they made a pact to withhold sex until the warring ended."

There was a stunned silence. No one stirred. No one breathed. After a moment, Clarice asked, "Did it work?"

"Yes, but there were some comical situations. The characters playing the men began playing their parts sporting huge tents in the front of their robes."

The women began laughing. One woman fell out of her chair and had to be helped up. Two women started stomping their feet in unison. One woman chanted, "No more sex. No more sex. No more sex."

Soon every woman was chanting. "No more sex. No more sex."

One woman raised her hand. "It won't work for me." She looked rather sheepish as she lowered her hand. There was a moment of silence, then the woman sitting beside her said, "No more potatoes. No more potatoes."

Clarice said, "Ladies, I think we've hit on something. Either withhold sex or potatoes, whatever works in your circumstance. When the men finally come to their senses and bow to the supremacy of the female—not till then will we once again allow them to partake of our gifts."

Clarice turned to Ophelia. "Did the women do anything to seal their oaths?"

"Yes, they sacrificed a bottle of wine."

Clarice looked at the stunned waiter. "A bottle of wine if you please. No, make that several bottles of a chilled house white. We'll sacrifice the first and drink the rest."

Clarice had to sit down before the clapping subsided.

CHAPTER 4—BARTERING

"Demas, don't say nothing about Tom to the Pike brothers. Tom's running from somebody, and we don't want anyone to know he's here. He's going to teach us to read and write if we can keep him hid."

"Charley, he'd teach me to read and write? Me?" Demas had a pitiful look on his face as he asked Charley again. "He'd teach me to read and write?"

"Yes, he said he would."

"I won't say nothing."

Chester came through the door. "Demas, you run the lines this morning?"

"No, Daddy, I've been bringing water. Charley says she's washing today."

"Okay, why don't you take Tom. He needs to start repaying us for all the trouble he's caused."

"He ain't been no trouble, Daddy. Yesterday, he cut almost a cord of wood."

"He did? I thought you cut all that wood. Boy, you turning into a supervisor?"

"No, Daddy, I'm a Demas."

Chester tousled his son's hair. "You take Tom and show him how the line works. He might find it interesting."

Charley gave them a canvas bag containing a water-skin and two sandwiches made with slices of pan-bread. "Bring me back an otter and I'll make stew."

When they got the boat away from the bank, Demas headed upstream. Tom sat in the bow and had his own paddle. Together they set a slow, monotonous, rhythmic pace.

"Charley wants an otter. We don't get many of them. Sometimes they get to chasing a fish and swim too close to the line and get tangled up. Sometimes we get big catfish."

"So, Demas, why don't you hunt for the game you need?"

"Our rifle's not too good. Daddy takes it, but he's afraid to fire. Most times he just lays traps. We switch off. One day I'll check the traps and he'll check the lines, the next day we change."

"How old are you, Demas?"

"Ten. Charley's twelve."

"You think you'll always live on the river? You ever think about living in town?"

"Naw, town's not for me. The other kids laugh at me cause I ain't got shoes and don't know how to read or write."

"Kids are tough everywhere. They say exactly what they think without regard for how it sounds to someone else or what kind of pain it causes." Tom paddled for a while then said, "You got any friends?"

"Yeah, there's other families living along the banks of the river. Sometimes the river overflows so if there's no high ground close to the bank, they put their houses away a piece. Then they hide their boats, so you can make it by their place and not even know they're there."

Even though the water moved slowly against them, they eventually made it upstream. Occasionally, Demas pointed out a path to the water's edge. Tom now understood there was a family up the path.

Suddenly, Demas started rowing furiously.

"What's up?"

"We got company and Charley says someone's after you, so we got to hide and let them pass."

"I don't hear anything. Oh—now I do. Where we going?"

"Back in here." Demas went around a tree newly fallen in the water. He parked the boat between the fallen tree and the bank. "Lay low. I don't think they'll see us."

Soon a barge came cruising by. There was some sort of steam engine aboard making a chug-chugging sound as the barge kept to the middle of the river. Looking between the limbs of the fallen tree, Tom saw a small cabin with a window on each side. In a chair on top of the cabin sat a man behind a large wheel. There were piles of items and barrels placed in various locations around the deck. He didn't see any other person.

When the barge was well past, Tom asked, "Were those the Pike brothers?"

"Yep, Jim's probably in the cabin. He's the one who does the trading. James handles the rig."

"Demas, did Charley say why she thought I was being chased by someone?"

"You talked while you were in the fever. Charley was up with you for three nights running. We thought you was gonna die."

"I see. Did she say who was after me?"

"No, you'll have to talk with her. Tom, will you teach me to read and write?"

"Sure. I told Charley to have the Pike brothers bring us some books." They maneuvered back into the main stream. "Do you know the alphabet?"

"Some."

"Okay, now's as good a time as any. There's twenty-six letters. Say them in groups of three after me. Two letters are said by themselves they're g and w. Okay say 'a, b, c.'"

"A, b, c."

"Hey, Charley. Your dad need anything?" Jim Pike stepped from the bow of the barge to Chester's rickety pier.

"Yeah, a tin of coffee, fifty pounds of flour, a pound of salt . . . wait a minute, here comes Pa. He'll give you the rest."

"Okay, but first, here's some yellow ribbon for your hair and I got a dog for Demas. He ain't much of a dog. Too small for hunting. Found him in the woods back home. Thought Demas might like a buddy. Think your pa will mind?"

"Naw, he told Demas he'd get him a dog some day. Guess he planned on it when he went to Brewster or Danville but then always forgot. Demas gets his hopes up every time Pa goes somewhere, but he don't say nothing."

"Hello, Chester. You having any luck with your traps?"

"Some."

"Charley started to give me your list but quit when I gave her a yellow ribbon. What do you need besides coffee, flour, and salt?"

"Better give me fifty pounds of hard-tack, two gallons of lamp oil, and a hundred pounds of shorts. She mentioned we need coffee?"

"Yeah."

"Well, that'll do it. Wait a minute, you got any hens?"

"Dominickers."

"Good, I got a rooster mighty lonely. Here's some beaver pelts for you. Real nice ones and one red fox. He's the reason for my rooster's problem."

"Fantastic. Listen, Chester, I got this little dog. You know somebody I can give it to?"

"Maybe, let's see him."

"Hey James, fetch that little dog." Jim turned back to Chester. "He ain't big or nothing. Not much dog for a man like you. I really thought he'd be a good companion for Demas. Chester, a boy needs a dog."

"We'll see."

"James, also bring that sack of dog food I stuck by the rope."

In a few minutes Chester had his coffee, a rooster had his hens, Jim had his pelts, and a little brown dog had a new home. When Chester carried his goods into the cabin and James untied and began to back the barge into the channel, Charley came as close as she could and leaned out over the end of the dock holding the little dog in her arms. "Jim bring me some Nancy Drew and Hardy Boys books. I'll pay you with eggs."

"You got it, Charley. See you in two weeks."

CHAPTER 5—SAINT BARTHOLOMEW'S

"How did you boys like the game?" Father Donovan O'Reilly knew the answer. He'd answered dozens of their questions after the Men from Dancing Deer beat the New York Hotshots. He'd even shown his boys how to field grounders, to shag fly balls, and how to step when swinging the bat.

Lacy looked into Father O'Reilly's blue eyes. "It was wonderful. Would you please tell us again about Babe Ruth? Lawrence doesn't believe he ever lived in an orphanage."

"Well, he did. That's where he learned to play ball in the first place." Father O'Reilly looked at Lawrence, who was now looking down. Lawrence kicked a rock, sending it a few feet across the walled-in courtyard.

Father O'Reilly picked up Lacy and put him in a wagon already holding several cans of paint, paint thinner, brushes, and empty galvanized buckets. "Lawrence, you grab one end of the ladder and, Tyrone, you get the other. Spencer, pull the wagon and, Terrell, you push. Boys, we have work to do in town."

The first store they went to was Creighton's Jewelers. "Mr. Creighton, I see someone has painted your storefront."

"Yes, they did. Gave me a choice of eight colors. Did it for no charge. I guess them boys want re-elected to the city council."

"Well, sir, me and these young men would like to paint your trim. It'll look a lot nicer if we break up that pretty yellow with another color. We could put sage green around your windows and door frame. Maybe do the down spouts of your water drain system. We're also not charging. We just want to do our share to beautify the town."

"I think that would be very nice, but, I'd like to pay you something for your time."

"That's not necessary, Mr. Creighton. The next time you're in church you might put a little extra in the offering plate. God would appreciate it, and you'd build wealth in heaven."

"In my case, it would be the Church of Christ. I'd be happy to."

"He's the same God. It doesn't matter which of his pockets you put it in."

"Mom, look—the orphans are painting Creighton's Jewelers. We already done it; did it last week. What do they think they're doing?"

"They're trying to improve on our work. I'll have to talk to your dad . . . see what he wants to do."

Johnston Baker's family was finishing their fourth storefront. Joyce, the daughter, was on her knees cutting in where the storefront met the sidewalk. Brad, the son, was up the ladder, while Betty, the wife, held it steady.

Johnston and Boyd worked all week washing storefronts with the city's fire engine. One load of water was enough to do three, sometimes four, fronts. When they finished today, they would have every storefront washed on the north side of the street. That got them enough storefronts ready to paint to finish October and to make it half-way through November.

Boyd wasn't married but had his girlfriend helping the Stanky family. They worked on the next storefront after the one the Baker family worked on.

"Boyd, anything funny going on with you and your girlfriend?"

"No, I don't think so. What kind of funny thing you talking about?"

"Oh, nothing. I was just wondering. When you gonna marry that woman anyway?"

"Not anytime soon. She says she can't fix potatoes. Now, I ask you, what kind of cook can't fix potatoes? She can cook most everything else but won't even try potatoes. I told her I'd help. I even peeled some with a paring knife."

"Did she cook them?"

"Hell, no. Tossed 'em out. Said potatoes were bad for me."

"Well, Faisal and I got another problem. Our wives have started sleeping with their hair up in curlers and some gooey stuff on their faces. They won't let us touch 'em. I tell you, Boyd, things are getting mighty strange."

"Hello, Father O'Reilly. That trim looks real pretty. You a painter too?"

"Johnston, me and the boys want to help. We thought this might be the easiest way."

"No offense, Father. The painting families only want to thank you. It does look better with the trim painted another color." Johnston Baker shifted his weight to his other foot. "Where's the dark-skinned boy?"

"You must be talking about Russell. He's gone back to his mother."

"She re-adopted him?"

"No, Russell wasn't up for adoption. His mother came by on her way to California saying she couldn't afford to feed him. Said she'd send him a bus ticket. When that ticket came, Russell was one happy kid."

"I see. Are all your boys awaiting a bus ticket?"

"Some are. Some have given up hope. Now that America has gone back to work, no one brings us their children any more. We're down to just a few. Some though, like Lacy here, lost their families and they'll be with us a spell. Lacy will be walking again soon. His family was the one who went over the cliff on the Pig Trail."

"Yes I remember." Johnston squatted down to where he was level with Lacy. "Lacy, you the one in charge? You giving them instructions from the wagon?"

"Yes, sir."

Johnston stood back up. "We're going to start painting the trim a different color, like you're doing. Hope you don't mind."

"No, we don't mind. There's plenty work for all God's children."

CHAPTER 6—THE HEIRESS

Emmett Irving was a bachelor. He was forty-eight and had never married. He put his career first, thinking he didn't have free time he could share with another person. A few years back, he tested the waters in the state gubernatorial race. He'd been told it was hard for a single man to be elected, as women voters thought a single man couldn't be trusted. He really wanted to be governor, so he looked around at the available women. He didn't find one to his liking.

As one of Raylene's regulars, he knew first-hand the advantages of the married man. Raylene was wonderful, but she wouldn't leave her comfortable lifestyle. She said it was all business. She also said she didn't believe in love. Deep down, he knew marriage to a prostitute was not in the best interests of any elected official. And it didn't matter if the prostitute was reformed, nor did it matter if love overflowed between both parties.

Emmett broke off his relationship with Raylene and cast his hat into the ring. There were six other candidates just from his own party. He did some traveling around the state and entered a few debates but couldn't garner enough support or campaign finances to continue. So he gave up his quest and slunk back to Dancing Deer and to his stymied career as the Marsden County District Attorney.

Emmett thought Raylene's murder trial would be the catalyst to get his career moving again, but Michael Jellico proved a formidable opponent and swung the jury to see things his way. Emmett had to agree. At first, he'd amassed quite a bit of evidence pointing to Bill Potter, the town banker and another of Raylene's regulars. But Bill's defense attorney took that evidence, wadded it up, said 'hocus pocus,' and pulled Sheriff Sherman Shodtoe from a hat.

After Jellico's theatrics everyone, including himself, thought Bill was as innocent as a baby deer and Sheriff Shodtoe was a weasel in the hen house. So Emmett terminated his case against Bill and charged the sheriff. After all, he had Jellico's machinations done on his evidence, other evidence supplied by Jellico on his own, and still more damning evidence he'd added after the first trial. That damn fool, Jellico, had once again been his opposing counsel and somehow managed to convince the jury that a third person, Evan Bonds, was the actual murderer.

Now Sheriff Shodtoe had been hauled to Chicago by the FBI and, in return for his help in bringing the Canneli brothers' crime syndicate to justice, the FBI was prepared to put him in a witness protection program and stay him from prosecution for any previous wrongdoing.

Emmett seriously considered leaving the state's criminal justice system and stepping to the other side of the aisle. He'd even considered quitting the law profession altogether. Then the committee came to his house the Saturday before the baseball game and said they had come to take him to the courthouse. He'd been nominated, not for the governorship but for the bachelor sale.

Old man Ridley's granddaughter ended up buying him for a pittance. She was the first bidder and could have started it off with the bid of a dollar but said twenty to freeze out her competition before they even entered the contest. He spent the evening with Adelle. Actually, he had a good time. She was well-educated, well-traveled, and well-off. Her grandfather, Torguson Ridley, had recently passed away, leaving her everything he had. She was forty-two, six years younger than he, and still had a young girl's curvy figure.

"Hello, Adelle. This is Emmett."

"Emmett? I'm not sure I know an Emmett."

"Emmett Irving. You remember, you bought me at the bachelor sale. Don't tell me you've already forgotten. I certainly haven't."

"Well, it's just that I've got so much going on. What with all the parties I've been to and the drunken brawls I've been in, I really haven't had time to think about you."

"What parties? And what drunken brawls?"

"Emmett, lighten up. I don't think there's an ounce of humor in your body. It's not necessary to take everything so seriously. What can I do for you, Emmett?"

"You can have dinner with me at the Ritz and watch a play afterwards at the Ritz Grand Ballroom. They have a comedy I think you might like."

"I don't know. That play is for tonight and I already have my ticket. How close to the front did you get?"

"Row twelve."

"Emmett, you must've waited till today to buy those tickets. I have a ticket for the second row. If I were to go with you I'd still want to sit in my seat up front."

"Adelle, are you upset with me for not calling?"

"Certainly not. I mean, it's only been a few weeks. A guy can get caught off his guard. Dragged from his home like that and forced to stand before every unattached woman in town, I can understand the humility in not having anyone bid for his companionship. It's a good thing for you I didn't have any plans for that evening. You might have been the only bachelor there not purchased."

"Adelle, I thought you wanted to purchase me."

"Good Lord, Emmett." There was a pause on the line, then Adelle continued with, "Pick me up at six."

"Thank you, Adelle. I'll see you then."

Emmett hung up the telephone. He now knew why he was a bachelor. He didn't have the slightest idea how a woman's brain worked. What's with her, anyhow?

CHAPTER 7—THE BALL FIELD

Rupert Calhoun started the Calhoun Carpentry Company a month after he and Nadine got married. It took one afternoon to get his possessions moved into Nadine's house, but it took thirty days of hard work before he had a place to put anything. The closets needed expanding and shelves added to accommodate his meager assortment of plaid shirts, overalls, and single blue serge suit. Nadine had been buying clothes to fit her new image and, once started, was like a fire hydrant stuck in the open position.

One month after their big day, he settled in. Now the chimney drew, the windows opened and shut, most closets had double rods, and the house was level. It was time to start the new company. His first act was to write a letter to his brother, saying Claude needed to come back and help take care of the business beating down the front door.

Claude thought Rupert was pulling his leg, but in a second letter Rupert said his company had been chosen to build the bleachers and concession stand for the new ball park. Claude gave his notice to the girls and headed home. He'd made a lot of money taking care of things for the girls, and now he'd help his brother manage the business they'd always dreamed of having. Claude was fifty-five. It was time he did something he wanted to do.

Claude had always meant to return to Dancing Deer. Managing a bordello wasn't the kind of work you talked to your parents about. When Rupert first announced that he and Nadine were going to get married and that Nadine was giving him the money he needed to get the carpentry shop going, Claude was upset. He didn't have the money to pay for his half interest, and he didn't want to work as an employee. He went to Fort Smith to work in one of the ammunitions plants. From there he migrated to The Painted Lady.

Now he had enough to pay for his share, and Rupert needed his help. He boarded the bus with three suitcases of clothes. He'd eventually have to trade his silks for overalls, his cane for a hammer, and his soft Italian leather loafers for steel-toed Red Wings. It's what he'd always wanted and he whistled a tune as he walked to the ticket window.

"Adelle, you look so lovely tonight. You look like you stepped off a magazine cover."

"Why, Emmett, what a nice thing to say."

"I know, I'm trying to mind my manners. I don't think I've made a very good impression with you so far and since I'm getting tired of my cooking and you're the prettiest woman in town, I thought it would be in my best interest to come across as more genteel."

"Good manners never go out of style."

The *maitre d'* sat them at his best table. Soon a waiter brought over menus and two glasses of water with a slice of lemon stuck on each rim.

As they looked over the menu Emmett asked, "Have you made any plans now that your grandfather has passed away? I mean . . . uh . . . are you looking to sell any of his property?"

"It was such a sudden thing. He decided at the last minute he wanted to build the ball field and give it to the town, but Mr. Jellico was busy with your trial of Sheriff Shodtoe and didn't get the paperwork finished for grandfather to sign. I went ahead and started its construction. I just told Mr. Calhoun to make it look nice. He got some pictures and we agreed on a bleacher configuration that will seat about a thousand people. It looks like its going to take all of grandfather's frontage. I'll keep the road back to the house between City Park and the ball field, but there won't be any frontage on Main Street for me anymore."

"Are there any other relatives besides you?"

"No, I was the only one. He had a sister but she never married and died two years before my parents."

"Maybe you should keep the land. I could help you find another parcel to put the ball park on, and you wouldn't have to give up your frontage."

"No, there's not enough money to buy more land and to pay for the construction as well. Grandfather was fairly well off, but from what

I've been able to determine, he spent most of his capital paying for my extravagant living."

"Extravagant living?"

"Yes, I've lived abroad for eighteen years. I spent five years in Spain, Portugal, and France. When Hitler came to power Grandfather asked me to come home. But I got bored and he sent me to South America. I've lived in Argentina, Venezuela, and Brazil. And, for the last two years—until I came back this last time—in Bermuda."

"I now understand where his money went," sighed Emmett.

The waiter came and took their order. Emmett looked through the wine menu and ordered a bottle of house blush. When the waiter left, Emmett looked at the pretty face of Adelle shimmering in the candlelight. "Do you have any other plans?"

"No, I've already laid off the two servants. It's time to start conserving funds. Its either that or get a job."

"Have you thought about getting married?"

"Now really, Emmett. It's way too early to start talking about matrimony. We hardly know each other."

"Maybe so, but I need you and you need me. I can't get elected to anything without being married, and you will soon be out of funds. It's one of those situations of convenience. Both parties come out ahead."

"I'll have to think about it. I'd always expected to be whisked off my feet, not picked up from kneeling."

"I don't understand. What do you mean by 'kneeling?'"

"Emmett, let's eat. I'm looking forward to the play."

"Okay, but here's one last thought. Suppose you stopped construction on the ball field? You could donate the land to the city and let them float a bond issue for the construction. Then you'd have enough money to start a business and never have to worry about money again."

"And if I decided to get married?"

"Then, the lucky person you marry could use your money to get himself elected to the House of Representatives or maybe the governorship."

"What an exciting alternative."

CHAPTER 7—FAYE

"Ma'am, there's no roads close by. You'd have to go in on horseback or by boat." The rotund sheriff reached into a desk drawer and retrieved a topographical map. She was sure good-looking: tall, red-headed, slender, and determined—damn determined.

The sheriff unrolled the map on his desktop. "Now, here's where the accident occurred. The last two passenger cars overhung the river right here." He used his index finger to point to a smudged spot. "If he fell into the river, he probably drowned. The fall was eighty-five feet and the river was flowing pretty good. Could've taken his body anywhere; there's hundreds of tributaries."

"But the little girl made it."

"Yes, ma'am. She was the only survivor found in the water. Everyone else drowned, eleven total. No, I don't think he made it. The little girl said he cradled her in his arms. His back hit first, cushioning the blow for her. She still lost consciousness. When she was found, she was half in the river and half on the bank. Since she didn't remember doing any swimming, we think they landed right there. His back would have been broken and, with half his body in the water, the strong current would have carried his carcass away.

"True, we didn't find his body, but there's numerous reasons. We have big catfish that could've gnawed him to little pieces or he could've been hauled out of the water by a bear. They don't go into hibernation until the first snow. We also got mountain lions and wolves. If he did make it to land, he wouldn't have survived for long."

"Sheriff, you've painted a gruesome picture. But I've got to try. Is there a guide I could hire to take me there? Since he was probably swept away by the river, I think a boat of some sort is my best bet. So, I guess, I need a guide with a boat."

"You get checked into one of our fine hotels and I'll make some telephone calls. Check with me tomorrow."

"Thanks for your help, Sheriff."

Charley put a portion of their coffee in two sacks. She took one and gave the other to Demas. "You go in away from the river and trade the coffee for eggs or money. You can't be gone but a couple of hours. I'm going to Granny Smith's house. We'll use the money and eggs to pay for the books Tom needs."

Demas worked the traps that morning. Something was setting them off and not getting caught. Must be some wily critter. He reset the traps and headed away from the river. The first cabin he came to didn't have children. He didn't tarry long. The old man he found on the front porch asked him plenty of questions, but Demas kept skirting the reason for his journey, saying only that he was on an adventure and soon left. During his short visit, he'd managed to trade a small amount of his coffee for a shabby beaver pelt and left the old man rubbing his chin with his thumb and forefinger. Water was now heating on the old man's stove.

The next place was where his friend Tarleton lived. Demas traded Tarleton's mother a cup of ground-up coffee beans for a promise of two dozen eggs by the end of the week. Tarleton said he'd deliver the eggs, as he walked Demas toward the path home.

"Your dog is a little small. What do you use him for?"

"Nothing. We just play. He don't know to be scared of anything. I have to keep a close eye on him or he'll wander off and get eaten by something."

"What's his name?"

"Tom said we'd have to come up with a real good name. A name he'd have to work at to live up to."

"Who's Tom?"

"Tom's teaching me to read and write. That's why I need the eggs. Charley's trading them to Jim Pike for books."

"Demas, you don't need to read or write. What you gonna use it for?"

"Don't say nothing, Tarleton, I wasn't supposed to tell anyone. Charley thinks he's running. He's real nice, but he don't know who he is. Says he can't remember. Daddy found him in the river and Charley brought him back from the dead."

"Wow, Demas, there might be a reward."

"I don't care if there is. He's gonna teach me to read." Demas and his little dog walked back with the pelt and Tarleton started making plans for the reward money he'd get when he turned Tom in.

Granny Smith promised to pay Charley two dozen eggs for her coffee, and the family behind Granny's house traded a bushel of pears. Charley thought if Demas had done as well, they probably had enough for the books.

CHAPTER 8—DANCING DEER SENDS HELP

Big Bear Radisson was glad to be back in his pool hall. Sure, he enjoyed the game. Heck, he enjoyed hitting the homerun that won the game. He also enjoyed the slaps on his back from the townsfolk, the free meals, and the cushiony way Kate Hamelin felt when she melted into his arms at the party, but that was then and this is now. Now it was time to parlay that notoriety into some serious money.

Bear's younger brother, Sampson, did a decent job running Snockered but it took the whole family to pull it off. Bear's baby sister, Sally, cleaned tables, his mother paid the bills, and his dad made the deposits and cleaned the parking lot. The first day back minding the joint by himself, Bear started to make plans. He had a sizable amount of money in the bank and business was booming. He thought he might expand. Sampson wanted his own place and Sally asked if she could wait tables for the tip money.

The second day, Bear scouted for help. He ended up hiring Sally and sent Sampson to Skunk Hollow to inquire about a second site. He even decided to pay his mother to mind his money and his dad to do whatever his mother told him to do. Bear thought he might just become Big Bear Radisson, the tycoon.

By the end of the second week, he'd hired a bartender and made an office out of one corner of his storage room. He was sitting with his feet propped up on a large keg of beer when Kate Hamelin sauntered in.

"Whew, smells like beer in here."

"Kate, darling, that's because there is beer in here—and out there. And people get clumsy when they've had a few. Sometimes they slosh their beer on the floor. We try to clean it up but it gets in the cracks between the floor boards and seeps under the bar, the jukebox, and the pool tables. A drunk comes in, smells the place, and don't know he ain't been drinking yet."

"You got a chair for me to sit on?"

"Here, take this one and I'll sit on the keg. You hear anything from Faye?"

Kate opened her purse and pulled out a telegram. "Got this yesterday. It says 'No one thinks he's alive. Stop. Hired a boat to scour the waters. Stop. Will keep in touch. Stop. Faye.'"

"What are you going to do?"

"I'm going to help her find him. I've already got tickets. I leave tomorrow morning at ten."

"Pretty fast decision-making there, young lady."

"I was hoping I wouldn't be traveling alone."

"And who would you be taking into the Appalachian wilderness?"

"Someone big, someone able to give me a sense of security, someone who would enjoy being alone with a desperate woman."

"Desperate for what?"

"Bear, go with me and I'll show you 'for what.'"

"Okay, but I'm not into that hanky-panky stuff."

Kate got up from the chair and sidled over to where Bear sat astraddle the keg. She leaned against him, reached inside his shirt and pulled out a few strands of hair, then kissed him on the lips. "We'll see how long you can hold out." On her way out, she looked over her shoulder. "I've already got your ticket. Be at the bus station tomorrow morning by ten."

CHAPTER 9—RUPERT'S PREDICAMENT

When Claude's bus arrived in Dancing Deer, he decided to walk to the library and leave his suitcases, then walk to the edge of town and see how his brother was coming on the new ball park. Nadine had a note on her desk saying she'd be back shortly, so Claude left his own note and headed off.

Claude marveled at the changes. Two groups of people were painting store fronts and a Catholic Priest was on his knees showing a group of boys how to play marbles. Someone had drawn a big circle on the ground and the clergyman shot his marble from inside the circle knocking other marbles outside the circle. Several boys stood around the circle waiting their turns. Each boy carried a sack holding the marbles called dates. Those were stakes for future games.

Johnston Baker walked up and held out his hand. "Claude, it's been a long time. You come back to help your brother?"

"Yeah, he said people were knocking down his door with business."

"Well, I'm glad. After losing the work on the ball park I thought his business might go south for the winter."

"He lost the ball park job?"

"Oh, Claude, I'm sorry. I thought you already knew. Old man Ridley wanted to build the ball park and donate it to the town but died before he put anything in writing. Now his only heir has decided the land is too valuable and stopped the construction. I think your brother lost a lot of money. He worked without a written contract, and now Emmett Irving represents Mr. Ripley's granddaughter. They're saying Rupert has to tear down everything he's built and restore it like it was. Emmett said he didn't have the legal right to do any construction. Have you not seen Rupert yet?"

"Not yet. Guess it's a good thing I got here to straighten things out." Claude continued down the sidewalk. He needed to know how far Rupert had gotten and how much they'd have to take down.

A few blocks farther down the street he passed a woman carrying a package as a gust of wind blew off her hat. Claude took a few quick steps and, just as he reached down to pick it up, the wind blew the hat another few feet. The second time the wind carried it a hundred yards, like a goose trying to get airborne.

When he finally returned with the hat, it was dirty, wrinkled, and the left side slightly water-damaged. Claude held out the salvaged hat to the woman, who sat on the curb crying.

Out of wind, Claude managed to gasp, "Ma'am, I'm sorry for the hat."

The woman stood up, holding onto the hand of Claude. She dabbed at her eyes with a handkerchief. "Don't be. I haven't laughed that hard since—since, I can't remember when. You, sir, are the gallant. Retrieving my hat like that shows me how seriously you consider yourself a gentleman. I am much obliged. Not so much for the hat—the hat is trivial—but for the effort . . . the effort was gargantuan."

"It was my pleasure." Claude bowed his head. "Claude Calhoun, madam. I hope I may be of better service to you at a future time. May I carry your package? It appears we're heading in the same direction."

"Yes, you may. But, I'm not going far. Mr. Calhoun, are you any kin to Mr. Rupert Calhoun?"

Claude and the woman began walking toward the ball park. "Yes, he's my brother."

"Dreadful business about him losing the ball park project."

"Yes, well, Mr. Ripley's granddaughter and that scoundrel Emmett Irving haven't driven him out of business yet. We Calhouns have a way of landing on our feet. We'll see who has the last say."

"I can assure you, Mr. Ripley's granddaughter had no inclinations of putting your brother out of business. I understand it was purely a financial arrangement, and your brother misunderstood the conditions. Anyway, I've heard Mr. Irving is planning on making some sort of financial settlement."

"Emmett Irving is a slithering snake. If he were to offer a financial settlement, it would only be to mitigate some larger potential loss."

"Does Mr. Irving have the same love for you?"

"Madam, I beg your pardon. It's not often I let a situation control my speech. Usually, I exercise more self-restraint. I hope I haven't offended you in any way."

"Nonsense. Everyone is entitled to their opinion. My name is Adelle Peterson. Please call on me. I would be interested in finding out how your brother turns things around."

"It would be my pleasure, Mrs. Peterson."

"Miss Peterson, if you please. But, you may call me Adelle."

Claude bowed again. "Then you must call me Claude."

Adelle took her package and turned on a narrow road beside the new City Park.

That evening Claude and Rupert tried to determine how much Rupert had lost. "Claude, it's not only the one bleacher I got finished and part of the concession stand, it's the arrangement I made with the sawmill. I've contracted with them to purchase their entire output for three months. I gave them three thousand dollars as a deposit and promised to pay three more installments of three thousand dollars each. It took all my money to pay the two employees and for that one payment. It was my understanding with Mr. Ripley's granddaughter that I would be paid five thousand for each section of bleachers as they were completed, another three thousand for the concession stand, and fifteen hundred for the outfield fence. She had other contractors for the plumbing, electrical, and chain-link fencing."

"And you didn't get anything in writing?"

"No. We always worked on a handshake. You know that."

"But we weren't working for so much money. If you'd finished, you'd have grossed almost thirty thousand. Let's see, there's twelve thousand in materials and no more than five thousand for your two workers, leaving you with a smooth thirteen grand in profit. Not a bad gamble. We just need to make it happen. Tomorrow we'll go see Mr. Jellico and find out what he can do for us."

CHAPTER 10—THE SEARCH PARTY

Faye started looking for Chief W.W. Wainwright in Carthage, West Virginia. It was the closest town to the train crash and five miles downstream. A train dropped her off, and she went looking for the county sheriff to see about continuing the search that had been abandoned the week before.

From the sheriff's office she came away with a topographical map of the area and the promise of a list of local men with a boat for hire. The sheriff was unwilling to restart his official search but promised to help if she decided to finance it on her own. She took the map, her luggage, and a passel of worries to a hotel downtown.

In her room, Faye sat in a chair by the window and started earnestly looking at the map. With her finger she followed the train tracks to the site of the wreck. From the trestle over the Oogala River, she followed the river downstream to the town of Carthage. She would search that distance of five miles first. Faye then followed the river as it snaked east to the Atlantic. In several places the river separated: one branch headed a little north and then further east, and the other branch a little south before it continued east. It was the root-ball to a rose bush. She would exhaust the river's main thrust before she started down any of the tributaries.

From her luggage, she took the few pictures she had of the chief. Most were cut from the newspaper in New York City. Why did this happen? Why couldn't he have made it to Dancing Deer and proposed? They could've been married and on their honeymoon by now. In his last letter, he said he was prepared to give up everything if she would marry him. She had been so self-centered, life was punishing her. She'd find W.W. and set things straight. She'd finally have a husband, a career, and a life—the whole ball of wax. But first, she had to find W.W.

After unpacking her luggage and arranging her toiletries on the bathroom counter, Faye put the pictures inside her valise and headed to the local newspaper's office. She waited a few minutes before she was ushered into a small office with papers strewn about and a cut-up board leaning against the side wall. This was where they pieced together the newspaper's final draft before sending it to the typesetter.

"Afternoon, ma'am, I'm Horace Honeycut." He stood and held out his hand. "Please have a seat."

Taking his hand, Faye saw a WWI commendation given to Second Lieutenant Horace X. Honeycut. It was framed and hanging on the wall behind his desk. There was also something written in parchment but the words were too small for her to make out. She said, "Mr. Honeycut, my name is Faye Spencer. I've come to town to find my fiancé, who was lost in the train accident two weeks ago."

" Are you talking about the cop from New York City?"

"Yes."

"I don't know how I can help you. We sent men for five days to search the river and both banks, from the wreck north of town to seven miles south. Nothing showed up. I personally think he got out of the water and perished in the woods."

"I appreciate your opinion, but I want to mount my own search. I think he's holed up somewhere . . . hurt, lost, and maybe a little disoriented."

"Okay, what can I do for you?"

"I'd like for you to run an article about him with a picture. I'm offering a thousand-dollar reward for any information leading to his recovery."

"And if he's dead?"

"I'll pay for that as well."

"All right, would you give me the information for the story?"

"I can do better than that. I was a reporter for the *Marsden County Meteor* in Arkansas before getting a novel published. I've already written the article." Faye handed the newspaper editor a single sheet of paper. "I also would like for you to make some posters that I can hang around town offering the reward. I'll pay for their printing."

"That's great, Miss Spencer. Anything else I can do for you?"

"No, I don't think—yes, there is one other thing. I'll need to hire some men to makeup the search party. I want to re-cover both banks of the river from the crash site to town. Do you think ten dollars a day would generate any interest?"

"Miss Spencer, for ten dollars a day, I'll lead one of the teams myself."

"That sounds great. I'll redo this last paragraph to include the fact that anyone wanting to work in the search needs to show up at the city pier. When does your paper come out?"

"Day after tomorrow."

"Okay. Saturday morning we'll officially start the search. Can you help me find some way of transporting the workers who show up to the site of the wreck? By looking at the map, I think it'll take them two days to get back to town if they stick close to both sides of the river. I'd like them to spread out so we can cover an area two hundred yards on both sides. I'm going to rent a boat and be on the water to keep up with their progress. And, I'll be paying in cash."

"Miss Spencer, you've put some thought into this, haven't you?"

"It's all I could think about on the four-day train ride from Arkansas."

CHAPTER 12—THE PENELOPE PINTA

The first man Faye talked to from the sheriff's list said he had a runabout and would be willing to take her all the way to the Atlantic for twenty dollars a day. When she walked to the boat dock, she met the short stocky man. He had removed the housing from his motor. Assorted tools lay scattered close by and black grease coated his arms up to his elbows.

"Is it sea worthy?"

"Oh, yes, ma'am. I'm just making sure everything's well-greased and in good working order. I've had to replace this little cog-wheel." The man held up a small brass cylinder with vertical ribs. "It's been on order for two months."

Faye looked over the boat. Fairly clean, it had a forward bench covered with a cushion having two loops of canvas. Must double as a life preserver. "Okay, Saturday morning we're going to the place where the train wreck happened and keep up with a search party on either side of the river as they make their way back to town. They'll stay out Saturday night but we'll come back and then be with them when they start out again Sunday morning. If they don't find what they are looking for we'll continue downstream Monday. The search team will stay in tents, but each evening you'll bring me back to town. I'm prepared to pay you twenty dollars a day."

"Yes, ma'am. That's the price I agreed to on the telephone."

"Then you better have your boat running and ready to roll Saturday morning at six."

"*Penelope Pinta*. She's not a boat, she's the *Penelope Pinta*."

Bear Radisson and Katy Hamelin arrived in Carthage the second week into the search. Faye had started with twenty men, lost ten, and picked up four when they made it to Carthage on Sunday. Monday morning she promised the men they could split the thousand-dollar reward if their search proved successful. Reinvigorated, the men set out downstream. By Wednesday, they were down to a total of six men. Six miles past Carthage, Faye called it quits. She had the search party brought back, paid the men their wages, and settled with the skipper of the *Penelope Pinta*.

As Faye turned away from the pier and started walking toward town, she met Bear and her sister, Katy. She ran to Katy and hugged her. With tears flowing down her cheeks she said, "I can't find him. We've been searching for eight days and he's not here."

Katy said, "Let's go back to the hotel and eat supper. Bear will come up with a plan. We'll find him. Bear can do anything."

"That's what I used to think about W.W. Now, I think he's put himself in a place where he's the only one who can help him." She looked at her older sister and then at Bear, who was looking at the ground. "But Mr. Radisson might be more capable than me . . . or maybe the three of us working together might be better than either working alone."

After the meal, they sat around a coffee table in Faye's room looking at Faye's map.

"Between the wreck and the six miles south of Carthage you've already covered are two tributaries. The first goes toward the town of Brewster and the second goes to Pauling." Bear held the map closer to the light. "I think we ought to go to both towns and hang your posters. If either town has a newspaper we could get your story published. I think we need to widen the search. Brewster is only," Bear used his finger and thumb to measure the distance and compared it with the distance scale in the legend. "only another five miles east and a little south. He could have floated that far easily. And, let's see, Pauling is . . . about seven miles farther northeast. That's also quite possible."

"Are there any roads out here?" Katy didn't understand maps.

"Yeah, but not many. At least, not many on the map. We ought to see if there's taxi service between towns. These people have to communicate somehow. How do they transact commerce?"

"The sheriff told me barges carry goods from town to town. He said they stop and barter with customers along the way."

"Okay, tomorrow I'll see if we can ride on one of them to these other towns. You ladies should check to see if there is bus or taxi service. Do you think the chief would have had money in his pocket?"

Faye thought back to her train trip to New York City with the chief. "Yes, he had a hard time sleeping on the train. He kept getting up and going to the john. The second night he slept with his clothes on, only taking off his shoes. I don't know if he took anything out of his pockets but, with his clothes on, he could pop up from his bunk and be down the hall before you could say 'I've got to pee.'"

"Then we need to show the ticket takers at the bus station, the train station, and these barges his picture. He might have purchased his way out."

"Bear, you're quite clever."

"Faye, I told you. Bear is a lot smarter than he looks." Katy looked at Bear and winked. Bear rolled his eyes.

The next day, Bear talked with two barge companies. The Pike Brothers' Floating Store and Burns and Axel, Barge Purveyors were the only ones working this time of year. He was told that during warmer weather a few smaller boats plied the waters selling what they could, but the two big companies had barges with heated living quarters and they worked year-round. Jim Pike said he'd be making his next trip to Brewster on Wednesday and from there he kept going to Danville and then on to Pied Eye. At Pied Eye he picked up a load from a textile factory and brought it back to Carthage, where it was shipped by train somewhere up north. Bear asked if he could book round-trip passage for three people.

"Mr. Radisson, we don't have proper accommodations. The cabin is just a small room. There are two bunk beds but no shower or toilet."

"The weather is still tolerable. If I could make it worth your while would you be willing to sleep in sleeping bags on the deck with me? We could let the two ladies have the bunks and I'd rig up a tent arrangement for the poop deck."

"How much we talking about, Mr. Radisson?"

"Six hundred dollars. Two hundred for each passenger."

"Mr. Radisson, I would want to be paid up front. I don't want to make the arrangements and then find, one day into the trip, the women want off."

"You got it. Is there any way I could come aboard before we leave to get everything set up for the ladies?"

"Yeah, we keep the barge moored at the far end of the pier. Just watch out for the porters bringing merchandise aboard."

CHAPTER 13—MEN IN A PREDICAMENT

Edwin Stanky had about all he could take. He and Gladys had been married for twenty years. It had been a good twenty years. She cleaned his house, cooked his meals, washed his clothes, and slept in his bed. She was a good wife. But lately, Gladys was going out of her way to make his life unbearable. The Stankys were one of the painting families, and Gladys was not working with as much effort as Edwin thought she should be putting out. And, on top of that, Gladys was not putting out.

"Honey, is there anything I have done to make you so disagreeable?"

"Edwin Dean! What could you possibly have done? Why, I enjoy painting. Of course our own house needs to be painted and no one has worked in the flower beds, mowed the grass, washed the windows, or taken out the garbage these past few weeks."

"Now, wait a minute. I took out the garbage two days ago."

"Yes, you did, but I'd filled up every container in the house and started putting what remained in your sock drawer."

"Honey, I work hard every day, and when I get home, I change clothes and we go paint the storefronts. They had to give us Boyd's girlfriend so we could keep up with the Bakers, the Satterfields, and the Obadiahs. If you'd work on them a little during the day instead of waiting on me, we might catch up."

"You want me to paint your storefronts while you walk around town looking for someone jaywalking? I don't think so."

"Now, Gladys, don't be like that. The other women are helping their husbands. Have you seen how full the pantry shelves are getting, and Thanksgiving is still a month away? Farmers are still harvesting their crops. No one's going hungry this year in Dancing Deer, no-sir-ee-bob."

"Well, I applaud your effort. I just think I should have been consulted on the issue before you volunteered my services. The other women are of the same opinion. We're only helping you guys so we don't have blemishes on our reputations."

"Then tonight, when we get home from painting, maybe you and I could—you know—go to bed a little early."

"No, I don't think so. I spend the entire time painting, getting madder and madder at you. If we were to do anything close to what you're expecting I might just bite your head off."

"Oh, that makes me shudder to think. Say, what if it rains? We couldn't paint if it rains. And. if we don't paint, you wouldn't be all that upset with me. What about then?"

"Well, if it rains, I would expect you to do the things you've been neglecting around the house."

"Oh, honey, what about the one thing you've been neglecting?"

"I don't know. I'll have to think about it."

Edwin knew he was treading on thin ice. His wife hadn't called him Edwin Dean since that time when he'd had the flu so bad his fever went through the roof. Gladys took the thermometer from under his tongue, read the number, swore under her breath, shook it down, and reinserted it. Each time the reading was too high. After three efforts, she threw the thermometer in the trash, saying it wasn't working properly. Soon after, he started shaking and going sporadically from freezing to burning up. During one of those freezing, semi-conscious states, he begged Lydia to hold him close. Lydia had been his high school sweetheart. Gladys grew furious and started beating him with a broom. Too weak to fend her off, he had to take a few days from work to get over the flu and to let his bruises go away.

"Listen, men. I've called this meeting to discuss our latest predicament."

"What predicament are you talking about, Mayor Bob? I've got so many problems I have to carry a tablet to keep up with them."

"Okay, how many of you men are getting regular sex?"

No one raised his hand.

"That's what I thought. The women are boycotting."

Boyd raised his hand. "I've never had regular sex."

Mayor Bob said, "Boyd, you're not supposed to have regular sex. You're not married."

"Good. So now all you characters are just like me."

"Worse than you. We paid the dues but aren't reaping the benefits. You haven't paid the dues and can back out of any arrangement you want with a simple shrug of your shoulders and then move on to other avenues of interest."

"Is there any avenue of interest that takes hold of you like sex?"

Harold Greenleaf raised his hand. "I haven't had any change in my sex life."

"You're the only one not participating in Bill's 'Sprucing up Dancing Deer' campaign."

"That's because I paid my losses."

"Yeah, but in winnings from Skunk Hollow fans."

"Say—that's it. The women are withholding sex because they're unhappy with us losing the bet and for making them help us pay our losses."

Everyone started talking at once.

"Wait a minute, gentlemen. We can't get anything done if everyone talks at once. The chair recognizes Johnston Baker."

"You might be right, Mayor Bob. This whole scenario started about the time I told Betty we had to start painting the storefronts."

"Yeah, me too."

"What can we do about it?"

"There's no way to retaliate. They say a woman has to have a reason to have sex, a man only needs a place. That probably works in reverse as well. A woman can give up sex for a reason, but a man . . . well, a man looks left, looks right, and sees lots of good places but can't find anyone interested."

"If we can't have sex I think we ought to do our best to act like we deserve good sex but are not all that interested."

"I think we should ask our wives to go to marriage counseling with that good-looking Father Donovan O'Reilly. He doesn't do a thing for me but the women get bandy-legged when he's around. He might be able to help us convince the women it's our right and their duty."

"And he might get laughed at as well."

"It's sure a shame there's no Raylene in town. She could make enough money right now to buy that apartment house she was living in."

"I understand they got a house in Skunk Hollow that provides—ow. Rube, that's my foot."

Mayor Bob stood up. "Gentlemen, I think everyone knows the situation. Each of us needs to determine the best way to react. If we let the women think their ploy is working, then the next time something comes up they find disagreeable, guess what'll happen? Let's not give in: no begging, no rhetorical comment, no arguing, no acquiescing. Let's play it like it isn't important. If anyone wants to put his own twist on things, try it and we'll discuss your success or failure at our next meeting."

CHAPTER 14—JELLICO SUES

Jellico arrived late. He had an appointment with the two Calhoun carpenters but decided he first needed to see how far they'd gotten on building the ball park. When he stepped through his front door, Brenda was pouring coffee for his two prospective clients.

"Sorry I'm late, gentlemen. I just came from Ridley Field. Another three months and you guys would've finished."

Rupert said, "That's exactly what we were thinking. But now, in another three months, we'll be bankrupt."

"I thought Adelle was going to pay you for the work you've done so far. You should be able to take that one bleacher down and the little bit of work you've done on the concession stand and sell it as scrap lumber. I don't think the wood's damaged much and, with the boys coming home, demand for lumber will be high."

Claude had a frown on his face. Rupert looked at his brother and said, "Emmett offered us a thousand dollars not to sue. He said we still had to dismantle the work we've done, but we could keep the lumber."

"Is Adelle Peterson Mr. Ridley's granddaughter?" Claude had fit together a few puzzling pieces.

"Yes, have you met her? She's rather pleasant to look at. I think Emmett's trying to latch onto her father's money."

Claude sipped his coffee and nodded. "Yesterday, right after getting off the bus. She didn't tell me who she was, just her name."

"I see. Okay, Rupert." Jellico turned so he was facing directly at Rupert Calhoun. "Have you received any money whatsoever for your work?"

"None."

"Did anyone hear you and Adelle discuss the contract?"

"No."

"Then I'd take the thousand dollars and get your work disassembled as soon as possible, before Emmett realizes how much the price of lumber will shoot up when price controls are removed. With the end of the war imminent, I should think anyone with a stash of lumber will find it similar to water in the Gobi."

"So you don't want to sue?"

"Oh, I'm going to sue all right. I'll represent the city. Mr. Ridley wanted the ball park built and donated to the city. He died before I had time to get the papers prepared. I'm going to sue because I feel like I let him, and the city, down. I'm not going to charge anything. And, besides, I like going up against Emmett."

Claude and Rupert exited Jellico's office and walked toward the library. They would take Nadine to lunch and have a strategy session.

A car pulled alongside and honked. The driver made a hand motion to them, reached to the passenger side, and rolled down the window. "Hey Rupert. I've been looking all over for you."

"What's up, Danny?"

"I need some of your lumber. I've been to the sawmill and they say they've sold everything to you for the next two months. I'm getting married and want to build my new wife a house. How about it?"

Claude stepped forward. "We're sorry, Danny, but that lumber is spoken for. We got several houses we're starting and we'll need all the lumber we can get."

"Damn." Danny had a weary note in his comment. Then he brightened up. "Where you gonna be building?"

"We're trying to decide that right now. There's several parcels of land available and a few lots in town."

"Then how about building a house for me, on my lot. I was going to build it myself, but you guys are much better carpenters me."

"You got a set of plans?"

"Yeah, got 'em from a catalog outfit."

"Bring them by and we'll see."

"Hello, is this Adelle Peterson?"

"Yes, it is."

"Adelle, this is Claude Calhoun. I was wondering if you and I could meet to discuss the demolition of Ridley Field?"

"Claude, I'm glad you called, but, I've turned all that over to Emmett."

"Adelle, my brother and I have been contacted by Emmett, and it's our intention to accept your offer. We're not planning on suing. Your offer is reasonable, and we've found other uses for the lumber that'll keep us from sustaining a loss on the project. But I want to discuss the timing of the dismantling of our work."

"Very well, Claude. Would you care to come to my house for tea? I could see you this afternoon. Say, around three?"

"That's wonderful. I'll see you then."

Claude Calhoun spent the rest of the day preparing for his meeting with Mr. Ridley's granddaughter. He polished his shoes, ironed a wrinkled shirt, and shaved—for the second time that day. He then slapped both sides of his face with aftershave and headed to the Ritz Grand Hotel and Ballroom. He wanted tickets for the jazz band from New Orleans booked to play for the weekend.

Promptly at three in the afternoon, Claude arrived at the Ridley farm. He was greeted by Adelle and escorted into her sitting room where she had a fire sending out slivers of orange flames through newly placed chunks of firewood.

"Have a seat, Claude. I have Earl Grey and a special English blend with a hint of cardamom from India."

"The latter sounds wonderful."

Adelle poured from a silver pitcher into two hand-painted pottery cups. "I was hoping you would call. I thought when you found out who I was and blamed me for the failed contract, you'd be angry."

"You're too pretty to be angry with. I just wanted to ask if it's necessary to immediately disassemble the work my brother has done or if we might have some time. We have another job needing to be done and don't have the manpower to do both."

"What other job do you have?"

"Danny Demeter just returned from the war and is getting married to his high-school sweetheart. We've contracted to build their new home. It should take about three months. But if you have plans for the property, we'll tell him and his new bride they'll have to rent somewhere for a while."

"No, that's all right. You build their house. I haven't made any definite plans for the ball park. I'll probably give it to the city, but they'll have to build it out with city funds."

"Thank you, Adelle. Would you write me a note to that effect?" Claude sipped his tea. "This is wonderful. I don't believe I've ever tasted tea flavored with cardamom. I don't suppose you purchased it locally?"

"No, I have a supply I brought from Bermuda. It was the last place I lived before coming home to take care of Grandfather."

"You lived on an island?"

"Yes, and in Spain, Portugal, France, and South America."

"Adelle, I'm impressed. I've only read about those places. I always wanted to travel but never had enough time or funds."

"Traveling in foreign lands gets old after a bit. You never seem to belong. Unless you learn a foreign language as a child, you can never speak it without a tell-tale accent. You're always treated as an outsider. I felt a big relief, and a sense of security, when I returned."

"Still, if you've never traveled, the adventure keeps beckoning." Claude finished his tea and set the cup down. "Have you heard about the jazz band playing at the Ritz Ballroom? I have two tickets for tomorrow night's performance. Would you accompany me?"

"I don't think so, Claude, but thanks for asking."

Claude was appalled. He'd never considered being turned down. This was going to be harder than he'd anticipated.

CHAPTER 15—MEREDITH CREIGHTON

"Meredith Creighton, please."

"This is she."

"Meredith, this is Claude Calhoun."

"Who?"

"Claude Calhoun. We met when Baxter Black's Big Band was in town. You came to my table and asked for my autograph."

"I did?"

"Yes. You asked me to write something nice on your table reservation card."

"I did? Yes, I did. I most certainly did. And now you've called. This is wonderful."

"Meredith, I have two tickets for the New Orleans' Jazz band for tomorrow night. Would you care to go?"

"You're asking me for a date?"

"Yes, I am."

"Mr. Calhoun . . . uh, Claude, I'd be thrilled to accept your invitation. What time do I need to be ready?"

"Is seven all right? Their performance starts at eight."

"Oh, yes, seven is great."

"See you then, Meredith. Oh Meredith, you need to give me your address."

Meredith was thirty and still living at home. Her father owned Creighton's Jewelers, and Meredith was his second-best salesperson. Of course, Mr. Creighton was the best. After graduating from college Meredith came home to find most of the eligible men at war. It was a common problem for the abundant single women. They learned to cope, to start careers, to build the armaments needed by the boys, to turn off their maternal clocks. When the boys came home they would re-wind and make babies.

She remembered Claude as a dashing man, tall and thin with slicked-down hair and a fashionable mustache. He was also a good dancer. She knew many women that night at the Ritz dreamed of dancing with the graceful man dominating the dance floor. Everyone in the ballroom watched while he danced with the newspaper lady. But he was considerably older than the man of her dreams. Still, no one had called and this might be the catalyst they needed.

When the time came for Claude to pick Meredith up, he arrived in a taxi. She wore a simple black dress with a plunging neckline. It was time to make a statement.

"Lady, you're beautiful."

"Thank you, Claude. Is there a special way of dancing to jazz?"

"I don't know. Can you do the Charleston, the Jitter Bug, or the Waltz?"

"Yes."

"How about the Lindy?"

"Yes, the Lindy as well."

"Then, my dear, we can handle anything they can throw at us."

When they arrived at the Ritz, they checked their coats and Claude's beaver hat. They were escorted to their table by the *maitre d'*. He presented them with menus and walked back to his station when the waiter came carrying crystal glasses of water.

Claude made small talk and glanced around the room to see if Adelle might be there. She was and, when he found her, she was looking straight at him. She smiled and placed her hand on Emmett's. This was more like it. Claude had momentarily lost his balance, but he was now back in the driver's seat.

Meredith looked around the room to see if there were any unattached men in her age bracket. She'd make the most of her opportunity and dump this old man when she found it convenient and had a replacement in hand.

CHAPTER 16—TARLETON'S PLAN

Tarleton delivered the eggs his mother had promised. Charley told him Demas left at daybreak to run the lines, so Tarleton tried to look around without arousing Charley's suspicion. He wanted a glimpse of Tom.

The river flowed from west to east separating the land. Demas' cabin was on the north bank and Demas' father had not cleared anything on the south. It was still filled with thick undergrowth, not a likely place for Tom to hide. He was either with Demas' father working the traps, with Demas working the fishing lines, or somewhere around their cabin doing chores for Charley.

Tarleton came in on one trail and left by another. The two trails covered the area north of Demas' cabin both east and west. A few paces out, he met Tom bringing two buckets of water from their well.

"Good morning. You must be Tom."

"Good morning to you. I am Tom. You a friend of Demas?"

"Yes sir. I brought Charley some eggs. You teaching Demas to read and write?"

"Trying to, but I'm not much of a teacher. I'm learning as much as Demas. I think he'll be back in a short while. He left early this morning to run the fish lines."

"I can't wait. I've got my own chores to do."

"Give me your name and I'll tell him you came by?"

"Tarleton."

Tom continued down the path with the two buckets of water. "See ya, Tarleton."

Tarleton didn't think Tom was a bad man, but then again, Tom didn't know himself if he was a bad man. Tarleton needed to go into Brewster or Danville and ask the sheriff if they had a warrant for someone matching Tom's description. He got to go into town several times a year but no trips were planned at the moment.

"Daddy, you like that coffee?"

"Yeah."

"Next time we go into town maybe you should get a large can. We could also get Mom seeds for the garden. If we started seed beds by the front window, we'd get a head start on the spring planting."

"Boy, what's got into you? You mostly fly by the seat of your pants. This is the first time I've heard you plan anything for the future."

"I just thought you and I could go on an adventure into town. Get your coffee, Mom some seeds, and me a pair of glasses. I can't learn to read till I can see without things being blurred."

"Tarleton, I didn't know you see things blurred. Belle, did you know Tarleton needs glasses?"

"No, first I've heard."

"Maybe we could muster a trip to the doctor in a couple of days. So, you think with glasses, you could learn to read?"

"Demas and Charley are learning."

"Okay, Tarleton. We'll see."

CHAPTER 17—READING, WRITING, AND ARITHMETIC

"Tom, Demas and I have written the alphabet ten times forward and ten times backward. I can even write my name. What do we do next?"

"Let's sound out the alphabet. Some of the letters are known as vowels. These are a, e, i, o, and u. The rest of the letters are called consonants. Each vowel has a short and a long sound. Take a, for instance. The long sound is like several a's in a row or the a sound in table. The short sound is like adding an h at the end to make it sound like ah as in saw. So now, let's say the alphabet. When you come to a vowel—that is a, e, i, o, or u—stop and we'll try to figure out the long sound and the short sound."

"Tom, this is hard work."

"I know it is, Demas. I wish I was a better teacher. I'm probably not giving you the information you need. We'll have to adjust. Each of us will get better as we go along. Demas, why don't we try to determine which letters in your name are vowels and whether they have long or short sounds?"

"Okay, d, e—hey that's a vowel—is it long or short?"

"Would it sound any different if there were three e's in a row?"

"Deee . . . no, that's what it sounds like."

"Then the e is long."

"And if it was short would it also end with the h sound?"

"Yes, I think so. Some words with a short e are step, led . . . uh . . . I can't think of any others right now."

"Okay, d, e, m, ah, s. Tom, the a is short. I can hear the h."

"Demas, you're pretty smart. You'll be reading and writing in no time."

"Oh, Tom, I hope so." Demas stuck his hands in his pockets, looked down, and kicked a little dirt. Then his eyes opened wide. "Tom, we got to go inside. Now, Tom. Come on, I hear the barge. Hurry, Tom."

Three days on the water and tempers had started to flare.

"I don't care if I am in a tent at the end of the deck and everyone else is half a mile away. This is no way for a lady to attend to her needs." Katy stomped back to the cabin.

It was now Faye's turn. She'd suffered through a similar ordeal when she was locked up and held for ransom by that Bonds kid. It was nothing new for her. Still, when you're used to being pampered, it takes a while to get accustomed to going days without a bath, with getting grit under your fingernails, with feeling like you're not pretty anymore.

"Katy, when we find W.W., all this will seem worthwhile. I admit it's aggravating right now, but we'll get through it and everything will be the better for it."

"I'm sorry, Faye. Of course you're right. I'm too old to play the petulant priss-pot. If we were to get a lead I think I'd be back to my old ecstatic self. Maybe this next stop is it."

"I doubt it. So far we've stopped thirty times and no one knows anything. They just look at us like we're stupid or something. We spent a full day in Brewster and nothing. Jim Pike says we'll be in Danville tomorrow and then two days later in Pied Eye. Give me a minute, then let's get the map and see if there are any roads we could travel. I think after getting to Pied Eye we should not return with the barge but travel over the few roads they got. We ought to hire someone to taxi us around, eventually getting back to Carthage, and then we can take another barge down the second tributary to Pauling, and then taxi back on their roads."

Bear sat on a keg of nails. He'd decided to give the women a wide berth. He didn't smell too good and hadn't shaved in three days, Then he went looking for Jim. "Hey Jim. I got an idea. How deep is the water?"

"Ten to fifteen feet in the center, down to four or five at the edges."

"How about me jumping overboard tied to a rope? I'd like to wash."

72

"Man, that water is too damned cold. Now, I could see it if we were in August or September but, Bear, this here's November. There's snow on the ground."

"The people in Sweden do it all the time. In fact, they go into sweat rooms and from there directly into water just above freezing. They say it's good for you. I'll try it once, for a minute or two, and you can haul me back in."

"Okay, but you got to be wearing a life preserver."

"That's fine if you got one big enough. I'll be right back. I'm going after a bar of soap."

"You should be lathering with lard."

"Lard?"

"Yeah, letting the catfish lick it off."

"Very funny. They'd probably take a finger or two . . . maybe a toe. I think I'll take my chances with the snakes."

"There ain't no snakes. They're hibernating along with the black bears."

Soon, Bear jumped overboard encircled by a hemp rope and the largest life preserver Jim could find. He splashed around, yelled a few obscenities, and lost the bar of soap. When Jim hauled him back aboard, Bear dried off with a semi-clean towel and put on a fresh change of clothes. He got a comb from his shave kit and detangled his hair. Thirty minutes later his hair had dried and stuck out in all directions. Jim laughed, but Bear said he felt fantastic and planned on doing it again the next morning.

James slowed the barge and, after the next bend in the river, pulled up to a make-shift landing dock. A little girl walked to the end of the pier. At her feet sat small wooden boxes stacked six high and filled with straw. James tied the barge.

A little boy ran out of the house, picked up the first box, and jumped onto the barge. "Jim, where can I put this?"

"What you got, Demas?"

"A dozen eggs. Hurry, Jim. I don't want Daddy to know. You got those books?"

"Demas, you can't read. Why do you need books?"

"'Cause, I'm learning to read."

"Okay, put them behind the cabin. Here, I'll get the rest."

Jim reached for the boxes, but Bear picked them up first and followed Demas. Jim went to the forward deck, opened a large weatherproof box, and retrieved a sack. He gave the sack to the little boy, who ran with it into their old cabin. From a corner of a dirty window stared a face trying to determine if he knew the giant man with the unruly hair.

"Charley, I brought you three Nancy Drew Mysteries but I could only come up with one of the Hardy Boys Adventures. Is there anything else I can get for you?"

"Thank you, Jim, you don't know how much this means to Demas and me. I guess we could use a tin of coffee, a pound of salt, a box of sixteen-penny nails, a bolt of heavy fabric, a spool of cord . . ."

"What color fabric?"

"Anything dark—and only one color. No plaids or stripes. I have to make pants for the guys."

"Charley, what do you and Demas need?"

"You got any paper and pencils?"

"I sure do."

"Jim, I ain't got nothing left to pay you with."

"Charley, you don't have to pay me anything. These are small things. I'll give you small things like them for free. Did your dad let Demas keep the little dog?"

"Yeah. Demas named him Radix. He follows Demas everywhere he goes."

"How about a book on arithmetic?"

"Okay, I guess. We're not very far along in our reading and writing yet. So far we've used sticks to write in the soft dirt."

"You let me know when, and I'll get it for you—no charge."

The little boy came out of the house followed by a small dog. He walked over to Charley. The little dog caught hold of the boy's pant leg and, raising its rear-end high in the air, started backing up, pulling, and shaking his head.

Bear asked the little girl, "Young lady, have you by any chance saw or heard of a man lost in the river."

"There's men getting lost in the river all the time. Sometimes a man's boat springs a leak, a man gets knocked out of his boat by having his back turned to a low hanging branch, or sometimes he comes too close to a bear fishing or gets between a mother and her cubs. It happens."

"I'm sorry, miss. This man would not be from these parts. He might be hanging onto a floating log, a capsized boat, or lying on the creek bank. I've lost a friend. Have you seen or heard of any strangers in the area."

"Charley . . ."

"Demas, take the pencils and paper into the house. Take Radix too." She turned to Bear. "No, sorry. I haven't seen or heard of any strangers around."

"There's a thousand-dollar reward for finding him." Bear handed the little girl a flyer with the chief's picture emblazoned over the top half. "If you hear of anything suspicious let one of the Pike brothers know."

"A thousand dollars. That's a lot of money. He kill somebody?"

"Oh, no. Nothing like that. We just want him back, that's all."

"Okay, I'll tell Jim if I hear or see anything."

Jim stacked on the pier the items Charley asked for. "Anything else?"

"No, that's all this time. Pa told me to give you four martin pelts." She had been holding the pelts all along. "And you can have this old one Demas found." She handed them to Jim. "Will these be good enough?"

"Yes, they're more than enough. Tell your dad he still has some credit coming from our last exchange. See you in two weeks."

CHAPTER 18—FOR HE'S A JOLLY GOOD FELLOW

"Claude, what line of work are you in?"

"Homebuilder. My brother and I are carpenters. Now that the boys are coming home, we've decided to start building houses. We're hoping there will be a shortage. I assume you work in your father's jewelry store?"

"Yes."

"Do you get along? I understand some people have a difficult time working for relatives. They always expect more and want to pay less. But then again, you have a vested interest. It may be yours someday."

"I have other dreams."

"You do? Would you tell me about them?"

The waiter brought the salads and a tray of yeast rolls. He placed a small cup of pressed lemon butter on the table and said their entrée would be out in a few more minutes. He then filled their wine glasses and left.

"I want to paint."

"You're an artist?"

"I have always wanted to be a painter. When I was a child I copied the Katzenjammer Kids' cartoons. In school I kept getting into trouble for not paying attention. I drew pictures of the teachers, my classmates, the classroom, recess. Everything I came into contact with, I transferred to paper. When I got older, I changed from painting what I saw to what I imagined. I started portraying people with frowns or in uncomfortable positions. Sometimes I had them laughing hysterically. Then I added action and unexpected colors. My father forbid me to continue and sent me away to school. I have a degree in business but can't imagine living a life arranging merchandise or taking inventory. I want out but can't figure a way."

"Meredith, let me propose a toast. Here's to dreaming . . . and more than that, to achieving our dreams."

At eight, the band was introduced. Meredith and Claude had finished their entrée, their bottle of wine, two glasses of a fortified dessert wine, and leaned toward each other huddled around a small flickering candle. Their hands cradled glasses of Napoleon brandy.

By eight, Emmett had been to the bathroom twice. He and Adelle had finished the house white wine and started drinking iced tea.

By nine, the band had played eighteen songs. Adelle had dragged Emmett to the dance floor one time, and she was presently watching Claude and his young tart do the Lindy. Every time Adelle looked in Claude's direction they were either quietly talking with their faces inches apart, dancing, or making their way to the dance floor. They did the Charleston with Claude slinging his thin young lady-friend over his head and between his feet, pirouetting to the beat of the music from one end of the floor to the other. When they jitterbugged, Claude got lower and lower to the floor kicking out his feet, while his sweet young date clapped, laughed, and giggled. Now, they were doing the Lindy again. Claude held her right hand with his left, one-two and a toe tap with their feet, push off with their other hands, a twirl—sometimes him, sometimes her, and sometimes both simultaneously—it was more than a woman could take. She stole a glance at Emmett. He yawned.

At ten, the band took a break. They had completed their first set, and it was time to seat a new audience. Their second set would start in thirty minutes. Claude looked past Meredith to where Emmett and Adelle had been sitting. They were gone. He and Meredith retrieved their checked garments and made for the door. Two taxis waited for passengers, but Meredith put her arm through Claude's and said, "It's a bit brisk, but we both have heavy coats and there's no wind. Let's walk."

Claude put his hands inside his cashmere overcoat pockets. Meredith slid her hand down his arm, into his pocket, and inside his hand. "I would not have believed a carpenter could have such smooth hands, or know how to treat a woman. Is it part of the curriculum at carpentry school?"

"No, you learn those things from paying attention. From figuring out what will make a woman smile. From listening to what she has to say. From devoting your full attention to her needs. From concentrating on the relationship and allowing her to tinker with it. I enjoy being with a woman who's having fun."

"Well, I enjoy being with a man who places me first."

They walked down the street past her father's store and continued toward City Park. The anonymous donor had installed lighting along the winding pathway. Piped-in music played in the background and the sky was filled with twinkling stars. When they entered the park they continued on a path beside a slowly flowing stream. On an arched bridge they stopped and looked down into the water. Submerged lights illuminated the ragged rock edges, the aqua color of the water, and the sleeping koi.

Claude took out his free hand and slipped it into his pants pocket. He pulled out a coin and handed it to Meredith. "Here, make a wish and toss it into the water."

"Claude, you are ever the gentleman. A woman's man." She gave his hand an affectionate squeeze. "Let me have that coin. I'm going to wish there were more men in this world like you for women like me."

"I'm honored." They watched the coin turn over as it descended out of sight. "I have a second coin. Let's wish together on this one. Let's wish you are able to fulfill your dream."

CHAPTER 19—MARRIAGE COUNSELING

Edwin Stanky thought his marriage was sinking fast. Gladys had not been civil to him for the past three weeks. He decided to see if the church offered marriage counseling, so he and his wife of twenty years could get back on the road of marital bliss.

"Hello, Father. Do you have a few minutes?"

"I certainly do, Edwin. Let's go into my study. I'll get us some tea." He turned, opened a door, and leaned in. "Mrs. Holloway? Mrs. Holloway, would you please bring a pot of your wonderful green tea and two cups. Mr. Stanky and I are going to solve Fermat's Last Theorem."

"That's a likely story. You've been working on that problem for ten years and you haven't done anything except run up our bill for paper and pencils."

Father O'Reilly pulled his head back and winced. "She's right, but last year I thought I was making some headway until I realized I'd made a miscalculation. When it was all said and done I was back to square one."

"Father, what is Fermat's Last Theorem?"

"It's a mathematical problem Pierre de Fermat said he'd solved in 1637. He wrote in the margin to a famous math book *'a truly marvelous proof . . . which this margin is too narrow to contain.'* Although all of his other theorems have been solved, no one has been able to solve this one. There's a substantial reward."

"And you've been working on it for ten years?"

"Yes, but I'm also here for you." Father O'Reilly looked intently into Edwin Stanky's face. He waited while Edwin mumbled his problem.

"Father, I think my wife and I need marriage counseling. We've been married for twenty years and our candle is growing dim. I don't think I excite her anymore."

"I see. Have you talked this over with her? Does she have any views on the matter?"

"I've tried to talk with her but she becomes aggressive and lashes back at me over the smallest of flaws."

"So, Edwin, what does Gladys think are your flaws?"

"She doesn't like painting the storefronts. All the members of the city council, and their families, are working together to beautify Dancing Deer and feed the hungry. She doesn't want to help me do our share."

"Anything else?"

"No. Well . . . she does trivialize my job."

"Edwin, could you come in with her toward the end of the week?"

"I can."

"Okay, let's see. Today is Tuesday. How about Friday morning around ten?"

Edwin rose from his chair and held out his hand. "Thank you, Father. We'll be here Friday at ten a.m."

It started raining Wednesday morning and was still drizzling when Edwin finished his shift. He went home expecting a hot meal and maybe a little something extra provided in lieu of dessert. But when he arrived he found his wife had played cards with three of her girlfriends all day and had gone to bed early with a headache.

He rummaged around in the kitchen. It was an alien place. He dropped a glass on the floor and was cleaning up his mess when Gladys appeared in the doorway and told him to get out of her kitchen. She'd fix something if he'd go into the living room and do whatever he did in there while she slaved in the kitchen.

In a few minutes, Gladys brought Edwin a plate of warmed-up food, left over from a previous meal.

"Honey, tell me about your day."

"Not now. I'm going back to bed. When you finish, put the dishes in the sink. Don't try to wash them. Many more broken items and we'll be eating off shingles and drinking from gourds."

"I'm sorry about that. It just slipped from my hand." Edwin folded the paper and placed it on the table by his chair so Gladys would have a place to set the plate and glass of water. "I talked with Father O'Reilly today. He wants to meet with us Friday morning."

"He does? What about?"

Edwin squirmed in his chair. This was the moment he had dreaded. How was he going to tell his wife, without her throwing a fit?

"He's going to start a group session on marriage and the family. He said we're such a happy couple he wants to use us as his example. He thinks you're the perfect wife. A firm date for his lectures to start hasn't been set, but he thinks it will be one evening a week, beginning in January. After he talks with us, he's planning on setting up a list of topics he wants to cover and enlisting participation from the other married couples in the congregation."

"Good grief."

"Hello, Father O'Reilly?"

"Yes."

"This is Edwin Stanky, Father. I'm afraid Gladys was upset with me telling anyone about our family problems. I had to tell her you thought we had a wonderful marriage. That you suggested the meeting to find out how we kept the love alive. I said you're planning a series of lectures on marriage and the family and needed a deeper understanding. When I framed it that way, she agreed to meeting with you on Friday."

"Edwin, you are a devious man."

"I take after my dad."

"Okay. I think I'm following your reasoning. You want me to paint your wife a picture of a man and a woman happily married and deeply in love, with her thinking I'm using the two of you as an example. And then, let her realize on her own where work needs to be done."

"Exactly."

CHAPTER 20—GLADYS

Gladys thought Edwin was pulling her leg, so she called the church office to see if she and Edwin actually had an appointment with Father Donovan.

"Yes, ma'am, ten o'clock tomorrow morning. Is there anything else?"

"No, thank you."

She needed to talk with someone. She'd call Betty Baker. "Betty? Thank God you're home."

"What's happening, Gladys? Your cat up a tree?"

"No. I'm the one up a tree. Ed and I have an appointment tomorrow to talk with Father Donovan."

"What about?"

"Father Donovan thinks Edwin and I have the perfect marriage and wants to use us as the basis for a marriage and family series of lectures."

"You and Edwin? That's the funniest thing I've ever heard. The two of you argue at the drop of a hat. When was the last time Edwin said anything nice to you?"

"Yesterday he told me I looked pretty."

"He did? When was the last time you said anything nice to him?"

"Hmm, let me see. I . . . I."

"Okay. There we have it. You can't remember. When was the last time Edwin gave you a gift?"

"Day before yesterday, he gave me a new pair of flannel pajamas. He said he could feel me shivering while I slept."

"He did? He touched you while you were sleeping?"

"Yes. He says he has to hold me in his arms before he can go to sleep. That's why I slumber so late in the mornings. I have to wait for him to start snoring before I can get to my side of the bed the night before."

"That's astonishing. I am talking to Gladys Stanky, aren't I?"

"Of course. Don't be silly."

"Okay, so he gave you flannel pajamas two days ago because he could feel you shivering. Have you given him a present lately?"

"Last year at Christmas, we went shopping and I told him to buy himself new socks and underwear on me."

"Did you pay for them? Did you wrap and put them under the tree?"

"No, he paid and since he knew what they were, there was no need for wrapping."

"What else did you get him for Christmas?"

"We don't buy each other presents."

"Now, Gladys, I know for sure he got you those gold earrings. And . . . and that book of poetry you keep on your coffee table. I opened it last time I was there and read what he wrote inside the cover. It was sweet."

"Well, yes. He did give me that stupid book."

"Does he get along with your parents?"

"Yeah, he and Dad talk baseball all the time and mom fixes him pecan pies. He told her she should get a copyright on her recipe. He's been known to eat half a pie in one sitting. And, you remember my younger brother Sammy. Well, Sammy got a little crazy on his eighteenth birthday and Ed had to go to Long Pool and drag him up the face of one of those big rocks. Sammy caught his foot in a rope and was dangling twenty feet over the water."

"Maybe, Gladys, you do have a good marriage, and we didn't know it, and you don't appreciate it."

At ten on a windy Friday morning, Mrs. Holloway ushered Gladys and Edwin Stanky into Father Donovan O'Reilly's study.

The Father held out his hand. "Gladys, thank you so much for coming. I told Edwin I needed a little help and he said you're such a wonderful wife that he couldn't imagine a better example for me to use."

"I'm flattered, Father. What would you like to know?"

"Everything really. How do you keep the romance in your relationship? What makes a perfect wife? You know, just tell me about you and Edwin."

"Uh . . . Edwin works all day, and I stay at home and take care of the house."

"I see. And when Edwin returns after a long day on the job, do you have his meal prepared? Do you do what you can to make him comfortable?"

"Sometimes. When I feel like it."

"Gladys, tell me what you like about Ed. Does he do things for you? Does he buy you presents? Take you places? Minister to your needs in any way?"

"Last summer he bought me a straw hat and sunglasses. And a new bathing suit."

"What was the occasion?"

"He had this elaborate plan for canoeing down the Buffalo. He packed a tent, a cooler of food and beverages, and a lantern."

"That sounds like a lot of fun. How many days were you on the river?"

"Just two. He expected me to do the cooking, and the coyotes howling all night kept me awake. I made him bring me back after that first night."

"I see. Did you get to use your new bathing suit?"

"Yes. Several times we came to a shady spot in the river with a sand bar. He'd beach the canoe and we'd swim or lounge on the bank."

"Sounds like a lot of fun."

"Not so much, if you get in a mess of chiggers while doing your business."

"No, I guess not."

"Has he taken you any other places?"

"Several times a year we catch the bus to Little Rock for shopping. He hasn't gained a pound since the day we got married. All his clothes still fit. Even ones ten or fifteen years old. I just keep patching them. I, on the other hand, have changed dress sizes a half dozen times. When we go to Little Rock, it's usually to buy me another set of clothes."

"Okay, let's move along. How do you keep the romance in your relationship? Is there a lot of hugging? Do you like to kiss? Does Edwin do anything you particularly like or, maybe, dislike?"

"Oh, Eddy is okay. We used to lie on the couch together and listen to the radio. But now the two of us won't fit. And, Edwin used to come up behind me and grab my backside, but not so much lately."

"I see. And did that make you mad?"

"I don't know. Father, could we continue this on another day? I'm so confused. I'd like to think about it. Besides, you haven't asked Eddy anything yet."

"Ed, what do you like best about your wife?"

"I dunno. It must be all the little things she does. I like to watch her when she's not looking. She sticks out the tip of her tongue and arches an eyebrow when she's concentrating on something. And, she spends a large part of her day reading love-story books. She's always comparing me to the dashing heroes in her stories. I know I'm not all that good-looking. I don't have the witty sayings or comebacks or even the thought-provoking detail. I'm just a simple man trying to make a beautiful woman happy. Did I tell you she hums when she works?"

Edwin Stanky looked at the Priest and then to his wife, who now sat on the front edge of her seat. "The men on the city council are doing several civic projects for the city and our job, along with three other families, is to paint the storefronts. It's been hard work with the cold weather and the wind, but she's out there with me every afternoon. She's not a very good painter, but she puts forth the effort and that shows me she cares. At first she got paint in her hair and on her hands. With wet paint on her hands she then wiped her clothes. I've had to dress her in a canvas poncho and a shower cap. After several hours of painting, we come home and, while I'm cleaning the brushes, she cooks our evening meal. We make our marriage work because we operate as a team. And she's my best friend."

CHAPTER 21—DANVILLE

When the Pike Brothers' Floating Store pulled into Danville, Jim announced they'd be there for the night. They'd leave the next day around noon with replenished cargo and galley supplies. Faye and Katy packed their suitcase and, dragging Bear carrying a sack of dirty clothes, they left the city pier for a hotel downtown.

"I could've stayed with the boat. Now that I've figured out how to take a bath, I'm enjoying the adventure a lot more. Course, I need a haircut and a shave."

"You look like a gorilla. With your size and the way your hair sticks out in all directions, you're scaring the children."

Bear dropped a few paces behind the two women. He'd been bathing regularly. Every morning he jumped overboard with a rope tied around his waist, wearing a life jacket, and carrying a bar of soap. He'd developed a procedure of turning around so the barge pulled him along from the back. That way he was more or less sitting in, or rather, skimming on top of the water. He lathered up, sang bawdy songs, and then turned around facing the barge so he could dip his head in the water, washing off the soap. Then, he turned again facing away from the boat. He'd lean back and rest his head on the taut rope and relax. He enjoyed the ride.

Being hauled aboard was another matter. That first time. James eased off on the throttle and Jim pulled in the rope, hauling Bear to the loading area of the bulkhead. Bear jockeyed for position and, with difficulty, pulled his massive body on board without a place to plant a foot. Katy tried to help until she realized Bear was completely naked. He'd lost his shorts in the swirling water. The next time, James rigged up a crane and, from then on, it was just like loading supplies.

When they reached the hotel, the desk clerk looked at the three bedraggled journeyers and said all his rooms were full. On the way to the second hotel, Bear suggested he go in alone to see if they had rooms. Both ladies were indignant at his suggestion until they realized they had been four days on the water without a bath, without shampooing their hair, and without applying makeup. At the second hotel, Bear came out with two room keys. He had rented a single for him and a double for his traveling companions.

The ladies took their room key and hurried through the hotel lobby to the elevator. Bear tarried, thinking he'd take the next elevator or maybe the stairs. After all, their rooms were only on the second floor and it was a close, confining elevator. The other passengers were mighty pleased when the two unkempt women got off at the first stop.

Two hours later the women met Bear in the hotel lobby.

"Let's find a place to eat, then while I'm at police headquarters you two can start posting these bills." Faye handed Bear a stack of posters, a sack of black tacks, and a small hammer.

Bear also wrangled a haircut, with Katy suggesting styling improvements to the barber. Faye checked to see if any bodies had been found or any strangers locked in the town or county jails or admitted to the local hospital.

By dark, they had the city plastered with pictures of W.W. Wainwright in a white dinner jacket and black satin bowtie. The poster said there was a thousand-dollar reward for information of his whereabouts. Anyone with information needed to contact the local police authorities.

That night, they enjoyed a delightful meal of fried catfish, coleslaw, and hush puppies. They took their time, savoring each bite, knowing it would soon be two more days on the water, with no decent cook aboard.

The women's skin had taken on radiant glows from being outdoors. Bear even looked presentable with a haircut and his facial hair removed. Katy put her hand against his face, her palm resting against his jaw.

"I was beginning to like the prehistoric look. You looked like a mountain man who took no prisoners. We women are always looking for someone to protect us."

"I might grow another some day, but not right now. It itched." Bear looked at Faye. "What'd the police tell you?"

"Only that the authorities from the train came looking and had already given them a description. The train offered a five hundred dollar reward. So now if he shows up, someone will pocket enough to buy a new house."

"Maybe one of those kit houses from the Sears and Roebuck catalog."

After their dinner came, Bear asked Faye, "How long you gonna look?"

"As long as it takes."

"Okay. I feel reasonably sure he's not between here and the wreck. So that leaves the roads and the river to Pied Eye. How's your money holding out?"

"I've got plenty. About eight thousand in cash and a letter from Bill's bank. We're not hurting for money."

CHAPTER 22—ADELLE'S NEW KITCHEN

"Emmett, what do you think about remodeling the house?"

"What's wrong with it?"

"Oh, nothing's wrong with it, but now that I'm doing the cooking, I thought I'd like a more modern place to work. The new stoves heat using electricity or propane instead of wood, and you can't buy an icebox anymore. Everyone's selling refrigerators. And I'd like to tear out these metal cabinets and have new wooden ones built. What do you think?"

"I think it's a waste of money. You have to use money like it's a resource. No frittering it away. Only use it when entirely necessary. The old stove and icebox still work and the cabinets still hold the dishes and glassware. If you want to buy something, you should buy a new car. The factories are going back to producing their pre-war products and before long new cars will be available again."

"But I don't need a car. The groceries are delivered each week and everything else is within walking distance. Besides, there's taxis just a phone call away."

"But, Adelle, a car says your somebody. It says you're prosperous—wealthy even."

"But I'm not. I received the bill from the funeral home and the cemetery association this week. I'm even poorer than I thought."

"Have you thought of selling the farm?"

"No, but I have thought of getting a job. I could be a school teacher."

"Adelle, a school teacher wouldn't fit the image I need for you to make. Have you thought any more about you and me getting married?"

"No, I have to admit that caught me by surprise. I'm mulling it over but need some time. Marriage is a big commitment. It's not something to be taken lightly."

"Okay, but don't take too long. If I'm going to run for office, I have to make application and start planning my campaign."

"I promise, Emmett, I won't string you along. Just give me a few more weeks."

That afternoon, Adelle walked into town and asked several people for names of local carpenters doing remodeling. She would have her new kitchen with, or without, Emmett's approval. There were several available, but the only ones anyone would recommend were Rupert and Claude Calhoun. She wrote down several names anyway and, when she returned, called the first two on her list.

The next morning, Adelle agreed to new kitchen cabinets from the first carpenter to grace her doorstep. Excited at the prospects of a modern kitchen, she opened a Montgomery Wards catalog and penned an order for appliances.

"Rupert, I need to buy some lumber."

"Can't."

"What do you mean you can't? The sawmill says they've sold you their entire production for the next two months and yesterday you bought an option to extend that by an additional three. What's going on, Rupert? You trying to put the rest of us out of business?"

"Now, Skitch. There's other sawmills."

"Yeah, but they don't deliver, and I ain't got a truck. And, besides that, gasoline's too hard to come by to make a trip all the way to Morrilton. What am I gonna do?"

"You're a decent carpenter. Why don't you work for us building houses? Claude and I have started one and have another lined up as soon as we finish the first. We'll pay you top dollar. You can make more working for us than you could on your own without lumber. You could be the foreman of the crew building this first house. We got a couple of new hands without much experience. They're good men and hard workers but inexperienced. I'd like to hire you to train them. I'd then start on the second house with another crew. Claude's lining up even more work. It looks like we're gonna need several crews to meet the demand."

"I'll talk to my wife. Say, if I came to work for you, would you also hire my kid brother? He's graduating from high school in May."

"Sure, I'll put him on your crew."

"No, you'd have to put him on someone else's crew. The kid thinks he knows everything already. I wouldn't be able to teach him anything, but he'll listen to you or Claude."

"Okay, If you'll come to work for us, I'll put him on a second crew. I'll be the foreman of it for a while but eventually someone else will have to step up. According to Claude, we'll have three or four crews by next summer."

"That's great, Rupert. I always knew you and Claude were the best carpenters in these parts. Now, I've found, you're also the shrewdest."

Later that same morning, Adelle's carpenter called to cancel the kitchen remodel.

"Miss Peterson, I can't get any lumber. The Calhouns have monopolized the market. You'll have to call them to get your job done. You might want to get in line soon though, they now have all the business in town. Me and some of the others are even going to work for them."

That afternoon, Adelle called the Calhoun Construction Company—recently with a name change from the Calhoun Carpentry Company. "Claude, do you think you could work in a small construction project for me?"

"Sure, let me come by and you can show me what you want."

When Claude arrived, Adelle was baking bread. The heady aroma spread throughout the house but was strongest in the kitchen where she had set up shop. She had Claude sit down at her kitchen table.

Wearing a colorful apron, Adelle worked while she talked. "Claude, I just can't cook in this old kitchen. I've ordered a new stove and refrigerator and I want new cabinets to go with them. What do you think?" She took a thick kitchen towel and removed the bread from her old-fashioned wood-burning stove. She then set it on a trivet in the middle of the table, leaving barely enough room for Claude's tablet of paper and ruler.

Claude salivated while trying to put his measurements to paper.

Adelle removed sweet-cream butter from the icebox and molasses from a cupboard. "Would you care to sample my cooking?"

"I don't know. Do policemen eat donuts?"

"You know they do."

"Same for me." Claude took an offered roll, broke it open with his fingers, and spread on a liberal chunk of butter and a heaping spoon of thick molasses.

"I have preserves if you prefer."

"No, I love molasses. Adelle, how did you get these . . ." Claude held up half a roll. "so flaky? They're wonderful."

"I took cooking lessons while living in France."

"Then we need to get you a kitchen worthy of your culinary abilities."

"Claude, I do believe you can read minds."

CHAPTER 23—TOM'S PLAN

"Charley, do you think this is me?"

"Hard to say, Tom. You're so dandied in the picture I can't tell. Did you recognize the man? He seemed awfully nice but he's as big as a barn. I don't think you ought to get in a fight with him. He's probably slow, but if he ever got a hold of you, he could throw you up in a tree too high to climb down. You'd have to hold on and see if it swayed close enough to the ground to jump off."

"What could I have done to generate a thousand-dollar reward?"

"You'd have to have killed somebody."

"That's what I was thinking."

Demas was looking at the picture. "Tom, I don't think you killed anybody. I think you're a gangster—or running from gangsters. This picture is from some big town. Somewhere like Philadelphia or New York City. See the shoes. They're shined. In most towns, at least in Brewster and in Danville, the streets are mostly dirt or cobblestone or sometimes brick. Only in a really large town would someone spend the time to shine his shoes. They got to have all paved streets and sidewalks."

Demas handed the flyer back to a stunned Tom. "Demas, if I teach you how to read and write, will you teach me how to solve puzzles?"

"Aw, shucks, Tom. I ain't smart."

"Demas, you don't give yourself enough credit. I've only been working with you and Charley for a few weeks and you already know the alphabet and how to sound out words. Charley is so smart she can read some of the sentences."

"Yeah, I know, but I think she's figured out what happens next and makes the sentences fit."

"Then we need more books."

"Tom, let's get back to you. What you gonna do if that guy comes looking for you?"

"I don't know, Charley. Let's ask Demas." Charley and Tom both turned to Demas.

"Okay, here's what I'd do. First, there's two trails and the river. So you got to have two escape routes depending on where he's coming from. And we got to have a warning signal. Tom, do you know what a squirrel sounds like?"

"No, show me, Demas."

"They go 'chink-chink', pause, 'chink-chink-chink.'"

"I'll have to practice it."

"Now, Tom, think. If you see him first you'll have to high-tail it right then. If Charley or I see him first we'll be the ones to sound like a squirrel. That'll let you know. He's not coming after us. You don't have to warn us, we have to warn you."

"Some day, Demas, I'm going to send you to college."

"Then I'd have a stash of supplies hidden along each of the two escape routes and some sort of map I always kept in my pocket so I wouldn't get lost. We could even lay some traps—trip wires or buried spikes."

"Demas, with you figuring the details I don't think I have anything to worry about. And what's more, it's a good thing no one's hunting you."

"Tom, if he comes by river you sneak out a back window and down a trail. Don't take the river. He'll have a boat with a motor and overtake you for sure. If he's coming down one of the trails and you have to go by the river. Be quiet about it. If he see's you, go as far as you can downstream till dark, then hide the boat. I'll find it. Don't go upstream. You'll be traveling so slow he'll overtake you traveling the river bank. He won't be able to keep up with you on land if you're going downstream. But I think your best bet is one of the two trails. I can even fix them so you'll want him running right behind you. He wouldn't be looking for trip wires if you were twenty yards or so in front. And I'll show you where they'll be so you can step over."

Demas picked up a pencil, licked the point, and started drawing the river and trails as far out as he knew them. "We'll get started tomorrow."

CHAPTER 24—THE WOMEN RACE AHEAD

Clarice stood before her minions. "Ladies, it's working. I got Robert begging for relief. He says he'll never make another bet with Bill. Any others have anything to report?" Clarice's eyes surveyed the room. "The chair recognizes Betty Baker."

"I'm not so mad at my John anymore. In fact, I'm proud of the work we've done. The town looks so pretty and with all the food we've put up, no one will be going hungry all winter. I say we think about giving in and getting things back to normal."

"No way." Suzanne Abernathy stood up. "Just look at these fingernails. It's hard work shucking and canning corn. Rube will never hear the end of this, not ever. I plan on making him pay till Hell freezes over."

Noise filled the room until Clarice picked up a saucer and banged it on the lectern. "Suzanne, you are one vindictive woman. What would you do if Rube says 'I've had enough. I want a divorce.'"

"Well, I . . . I'd tell him to take a hike. I wouldn't agree to it."

"A judge might say he had reasonable cause." Clarice looked out over the heads turned her way. "I think we have to decide at what point we've gotten our revenge. How much do we want the men to grovel?"

A wild clamor arose, with hands raised in every corner. Clarice continued, "When the men acknowledge their defeat and we've unequivocally shown where the power really is, only then should we let them back into our beds. I, for one, have enjoyed throwing my weight around, but I also think we don't want to overplay the game. What we need to decide today is how much more aggravation do we want to exact? Anyone else want to express an opinion?"

Summer Satterfield raised her hand. "George is panting at the bit. I asked him to take me to the movies last weekend. We saw that new Garbo film. George thinks she's hot, maybe the most beautiful woman in the world. I told him it was just the sultry way she talked and the exaggerated way she swayed her hips. He laughed until I started mimicking her style. He immediately began following me around like a puppy. Yesterday he brought me flowers."

"That's good, Summer. Anyone else making headway?"

Ophelia Obadiah stood beside her chair. "I don't know what to make of Faisal's behavior. Earlier this week, he received a package from New Orleans. I steamed it open and found four glass bottles with cork stoppers. They were from Little Egypt's Love Potion Shop. A copy of his order blank was enclosed and a catalog. They sell aphrodisiacs."

The room was completely quiet. Then everyone started talking at the same time. Clarice banged on her lectern until the cacophony eased a bit and said, "Tell us what happened."

"Yeah. And I want to see that catalog."

"Nothing's happened yet. I poured everything but the powdered rhino horn down the kitchen drain. I couldn't believe he'd be trying to sneak that disgusting stuff into my food. I refilled with items from my cupboard. In one I put brown sugar. In another I put wheat flour with capers and dried pimentos. In the third I cracked black peppercorns and mixed in powdered clove and spearmint. I now expect to find some interesting flavors sprinkled over my food."

"What are you planning on doing with the powdered rhino horn?"

"I looked it up in the catalog. It's a male enlargement concoction. And so expensive I couldn't bear to dispose of it. I mean, what if it works?"

"And, just what is it supposed to do?"

"It changes a short garden hose into one used by a fire truck."

"Okay, anybody else?"

Boyd's girlfriend raised her hand. "A couple of times a week I go to Boyd's house to cook his supper. He's not had any potatoes since we started this charade and lately he's quit asking for them. But wait . . . let me go back up a little. Several weeks ago, I was toying with him. We were on the swing and I had a banana. I slowly pulled down the peeling and proceeded to lick it. I could see I had his attention. I mean, I really had his attention."

"Go on. What happened next?"

"He ran into the house and locked himself in the bedroom. I couldn't get him to come out until I'd finished preparing the meal. I really thought about frying potatoes for the poor guy but stood fast. We didn't talk about the banana."

Gladys raised her hand. "Eddy told Father Donovan I was the perfect wife."

"He did? That's a hoot. Everyone knows how you treat Edwin."

"Yeah, when Jerry and I argue he says 'Now, don't be like Gladys.'"

"You're kidding, right? He really didn't say that to the Father?"

"Yes, he did."

"Gladys, he's pulling your leg. No one in their right mind would think you're the perfect wife. That's the funniest thing I've ever heard."

Everyone in the room but Gladys was laughing. She ran out the door crying.

CHAPTER 25—TARLETON GETS GLASSES

"Daddy, do we have to get the glasses first?"

"Tarleton, that's why we came to town. We have to see how much they're going to cost before we know how much we can spend on supplies. We got a good price for the hogs and after buying the glasses, I want to know if I'll have a little something left to buy your mother a Christmas present."

On the square in downtown Brewster, Tarleton's father found an eye doctor. When they entered, a bell on the door tinkled. No one was sitting at the desk, so they sat in two empty chairs. In a moment, a man came through a curtain and left through the front door. He was followed by a man wearing a white smock.

"May I help you?"

"Yeah . . . uh, yes, sir. My boy wants to have his vision checked. He thinks he might need glasses."

The man in the apron turned to Tarleton. "Have you had any headaches?"

"No."

"Blurred vision?"

"I think so."

"Good, step in here and we'll see what can be done."

Two hours later they emerged from the eye doctor's office. Tarleton sported a pair of glasses with thick black rims and his dad sported a leather wallet with twenty dollars missing. "Now, tell me, Tarleton, how you planning on teaching yourself to read?"

"I'll have to get with Demas. He says he's already mastered the alphabet and can sound out some words. Maybe we could get me some books—real easy books."

"That's an idea. We'll go to the general store and see what they got."

Across the street was Brewster's major store. It sold everything from dynamite to dominoes. "I need to see what fabrics you got. My wife likes to make her clothes, and I'll need a new pair of scissors, a package of needles, a thimble, buttons, and thread to match the fabric."

"Yes, sir, right this way."

"Tarleton, you stay close. You hear me?"

"Yes, Daddy. I ain't going nowhere."

Tarleton walked over to the bulletin board. His eyes lit up as big as door knobs when he saw the poster of the dandy in the white sport coat. He snatched it off the board and ran to his dad.

"Daddy? Daddy, what does this say?" Tarleton held out the poster.

"Uh . . . Let me see. It says this man is Wayne Wainwright and someone's offering a thousand dollars to anyone who knows where he is."

"Daddy, I know where he is."

"Tarleton, you don't know where he is. What you been drinking, boy?"

"I do too. Does it say who I'm supposed to tell?"

"Yeah, the police."

Tarleton looked for help from the salesman. "Quick, mister. Where's the police?"

"Across the street and down to the corner, in the courthouse . . ." Tarleton shot out the door. "is the sheriff's office, but you'll have to go two blocks south to find the police." He was talking to a vacant spot. He turned to Tarleton's father. "The railroad's been looking for that man for weeks. A few days back two ladies and the biggest man I ever saw came in and tacked up that poster. If your boy does know where he is, he better play it smart and not try to capture him hisself. For a thousand dollars, the man's got to have killed a dozen or more."

The salesman helped Tarleton's father with his purchase and loaded everything in the back of an old pickup, along with the supplies he'd bought with most of his remaining money. Tarleton's dad then went looking for his son.

"I'm telling you, I know where this man is but I ain't saying where exactly until I get some proof I'll get paid."

"Sonny, this reward is offered by an individual. We can't make it good or even vouch for it. You got to take that up with her."

"How do I get in touch with her?"

"You sure this is the right guy?"

"Not one hundred percent, but reasonably sure."

"Okay, let me go ask the chief. I think he talked with the woman."

Soon two policemen walked toward Tarleton. The one leading the way pulled up a chair opposite and sat astraddle it with his hands folded on the chair's back. "You've seen a stranger that looks like the man in the picture?"

"Yes, sir."

"What makes you think he's the same man?"

"Well, the man I've seen is called Tom and he don't know who he is or where he come from."

"Okay, but does he look like this man?"

"No, not exactly. He now has a beard and his hair is pulled back and tied with a yellow ribbon."

"All right, tell me where he is and I'll make sure you get the reward."

"No, that won't work. You tell me how I can get ahold of the lady, and I'll tell her when I've got the money."

"All I can say is that the newspaper guy in Carthage—I think his name is Honeycut—has ramrodded the entire operation. If you want my opinion, I think he's trying to generate business for his paper. I've got his address. Here. You want to write this down."

"I'm his dad. Give me the paper. I'll write it down."

Back on the street, Tarleton said, "Daddy, we need to write Mr. Honeycut a letter and mail it before we head home."

"Okay, let's go back to the general store and buy some paper and an envelope."

"No, we need to find a different store. Only one person's going to get that reward and there's probably people already asking about us at that store."

"If you're so all-fired sure your Tom is the man, maybe we should telegraph this newspaper guy."

CHAPTER 26—BEAR CLEARS HIS HEAD

"Oh, there was an old woman from Nantucket. Who threw . . ."

"Bear Radisson, if you sing that dirty song one more time, I'm going to cut the rope and leave you for the catfish."

"Kate, darling. Why don't you jump in here with me? It ain't all that cold after you've been in it for a minute."

"I've been thinking about it, but it looks awfully cold to me. There's still snow in places from last week, for Gods sakes." Katy stretched, "You still got that bar of soap?"

"Yeah, you got a bathing suit?"

"No."

"You gonna do the desperate woman thing?"

"Maybe."

"Have James ease off the throttle and Jim can pull me around."

Ten minutes later, Katy wore a life preserver and very little else. She was also tied to Bear, who was tied to the end of a long rope, tied to a cleat on the bulkhead. Kate positioned herself with her back to Bear and between his legs. Bear's back was to the boat and they skimmed along at a decent clip. He dripped water from cupped hands over Katy's hair, then took the bar of soap and lathered it. She slid down the rope a few feet until she could turn around and stick her head under water, holding her nose. After washing off the soap, she let Bear pull her back to the previous position and held out her hand for the soap.

"Put this loop on your wrist. I was losing so many bars I had to start cutting a hole in their middle and threading through a small rope. I was fast becoming the Pike's best customer for soap."

Katy shivered as she washed. Through chattering teeth she said, "You say you get used to this?"

"Yeah." Bear watched Katy as she rubbed her arms and legs with the soap. "Say, Kate. I've got a question. Can a person teach himself to read from a book?"

"I wouldn't think so. Someone would have to show him how to sound out the words first."

"That's what I was thinking. Two days before Danville, we stopped at this shack and Jim gave this little girl and boy a sack of books. They said they were teaching themselves to read and write. I've been mulling this over in my mind and can't for the life of me figure out how they're doing it."

"You need to ask Faye. Maybe she's got an idea." Katy squirmed, trying to keep from getting splashed in the face. "Bear, I'm mighty cold. Can I crawl up in your lap?"

"Kate, have you noticed how Jim and Faye have set up chairs next to the kerosene heater? We must be making a spectacle. And, lady, you're not wearing much clothing."

"I know. I think it's exciting. What do you think?"

"I think it's pretty damn exciting myself. But we got to get back and get dressed before your reputation gets shot to hell or you freeze."

The crane dumped Katy and Bear at the feet of Jim and Faye. Faye handed her sister a towel while Bear ran to his sleeping bag and stash of clean clothes. In a few minutes they sat in a circle enjoying the warmth of a large tent heater. Faye handed out tuna-fish sandwiches.

"Faye, how does someone teach themselves to read and write? Can it be done by a book?"

"I don't think so."

Bear turned to Jim. "You remember that little girl and boy who gave you eggs for a sack of books? They said they were learning to read and write."

"I know. Now that I think about it, it does seem strange. I gave them that little dog last time through. I was glad Chester let Demas keep it. Chester can be difficult at times. His wife died a few years back, and now he drinks a lot. If it weren't for Charley keeping things together— well, I don't know what would happen. She seems to have a level head. What did Demas say he named the dog?"

"Radix."

Faye jerked her head around. "What's the dog's name?"

"The little boy said . . . no, the little girl said he named it Radix."

"We got to go back." Faye jumped up from her chair. "That's where W.W. is. Radix is the name of the mayor of New York City. He offered W.W. the job of police chief. Jim turn this thing around."

"I can't do that. Pied Eye is one more day out, and then we got to load up a shipment of textiles to take back to Carthage."

"I'll pay you three thousand dollars."

Jim stood up. "James." He walked over to the ladder leading up to where James was sitting. "James, find a wide place and turn her around. We got to go back to Chester's place above Danville."

When he returned, Faye had questions. "Tell me about this family."

"Not much to tell. Chester and his sweetheart got married and built that shack on the water's edge. Chester don't work much. Runs a line and some traps. They got two children. Then one day when he went into town for supplies, she got bit by a snake and died. He blamed himself for not being there and now gets crazy drunk whenever he's got extra money. He sells pelts and souvenir catfish."

"Souvenir catfish?"

"Yeah, he's caught some of the biggest ever landed. They're not so good to eat so he hauls them into town and sells them to people traveling through. Sometimes they only want their picture taken holding 'em up. Others pay him to dress 'em out and pack the fillets on ice. He then takes his money and blows it on booze. Demas is the boy, and he's a little slow. Charley is a tough little girl, but neither can read or write. There's no school out there. It's a common problem."

CHAPTER 28—HORACE HONEYCUT

Horace Honeycut walked over with the telegram to a window. "Someone's found that New York policeman. He says to bring the money to Farm Road 1265, two miles south of its intersection with Farm Road 2130."

Honeycut called the hotel where Miss Spencer had set up her headquarters and found she had checked out, saying she'd be back in a few days. She had left a suitcase to be picked up later. Horace mulled over the situation and eventually gathered John, his cameraman, and Cameron, the town bully. They headed to the location on the telegram in Honeycut's Dodge pickup.

"Hello, my name is Honeycut. Are you the one who sent the telegram saying you've seen Wainwright?"

"No, my boy did. Come in. I'll get him."

Tarleton's mother hurried down the worn path leading to the stable where Tarleton did most of his chores. "Son, you got visitors. You sure you've seen this man they're looking for?"

"I think so. If he's the one, they're going to give me a thousand dollars."

They headed back but Tarleton broke into a run and was in the house before his mother.

"All right, young man, where did you see him?"

"You got my money?"

"If he's the man, you'll get your money. I promise."

"Let me think." Tarleton sat in a chair. "He ain't going nowhere. I can wait."

"What? You're not going to tell us until you have the money? What if he's not the right guy?"

"I'll give the money back."

"Sonny, that's not the way things work. You give us the guy and, if he's the man, you get your money, not before."

"Let's meet halfway. You give me half the money now, and then we'll see if he's the right man."

"Ma'am, can you help me out here?"

"Sorry, mister. The boy takes after his grandpa. It's his call."

"What's your name, boy?"

"Tarleton."

"Okay, Tarleton. Let's dicker. I ain't got five hundred. The lady who's offering to pay will be the one shelling out. I left her a note. According to the hotel in Carthage, she checks back every once in awhile and they have some of her luggage. If we could take him back or, at least, get his picture, I could sell all the papers I could print and you'd surely get your money."

He looked at his young adversary. The boy folded his arms confrontationally. He nodded occasionally to let Honeycut know he understood, but since he was holding all the cards he was not going to dicker much.

"Look, what I've got is a Dodge truck. How about I give you the keys and, if he's the man, you'll get your money and you can give me back the truck. But we'll need a ride in it back to town. Now, is that good enough?"

"Yep." Tarleton held out his hand.

"John, go get the keys. They're in the ignition." The cameraman dashed out and returned in a minute with the keys. "You don't need the key to my house or the newspaper." He disassembled the key ring and held up the largest key with 'Dodge' embossed on its shank.

Honeycut handed over the key and held out his hand to complete the deal with a handshake.

"Now will you tell me where he is?"

"I'll have to take you. He's staying with a friend of mine and they ain't on a road but on the river. It's an hour's walk."

Tom didn't know why he didn't have any outdoor savvy. Demas had to teach him how to use the ax, to counter the weight by carrying two buckets of water instead of one, to paddle a canoe, to bank a fire, to track game, to skin and filet a catfish, and to bait and run the lines and traps. It had been an eventful two months and in return he'd been teaching Demas and Charley to read and write. He still had no recollection of anything prior to being rescued. To him, home was a small shack on the river's edge. He worked hard so he'd not be asked to leave. He didn't have anywhere to go. That morning he was cutting firewood.

Tom picked up a fat log and sat it upright on a flat stump. He raised the ax high over his head and was about to change directions, bringing it down to split the log when he heard a creak. It sounded like a slender piece of green wood pinched between two heavier pieces of green wood, was being pulled over a hollow noise box.

Tom dropped the ax and ran for the cabin. Along the way, he made the sound of a squirrel. "Chink, chink." A pause. "Chink, chink, chink."

He stopped at the cabin door long enough for Charley to hand him a sack of food and a thermos of water. He then shot down a second path clutching the bag. He reached a lookout point where he had a good view of the cabin and waited to see who would come along the path past the woodpile.

Three men and Tarleton walked up to Charley's door and knocked. Charley let them in. A few minutes later the door opened and all four started down the path he'd just taken.

"Damn. Must've beat it out of her. Okay, Demas, its showtime."

CHAPTER 29—THE WOMEN STUMBLE

Clarice decided she might better check her relationship with Bob. "Honey, what do you think about these shoes?"

She came out of the bedroom wearing red high heels with a tiny red strap wrapped around each ankle. Above the shoes was a long length of silky smooth leg to sexy red panties trimmed with white lace. Above the panties was a taut stomach stretching to a new red bra with the wires bent, pushing her cleavage out at the top.

Clarice watched her husband as she walked to his chair by the radio. She saw the bulge in his throat dip as he swallowed. Perspiration beaded on his forehead.

"It depends on what you're wearing them with. Red doesn't go with everything, not like black. And it would have to be an evening dress. There's no way you could wear them to go—say Christmas shopping."

"I thought I'd wear them when you light the Christmas tree at City Park."

"Yes, I can see it now. The paper will have to print a picture of you because the photographer forgot to take a picture of me. Maybe you should run for mayor next term. You'd be the prettiest mayor in Arkansas."

"You know, I just might."

"You're welcome to it. It's been nothing but a headache for me."

"So. What do you like about the shoes?"

"Hmm . . . walk around some more." Bob's eyes followed his wife. She crossed the room to her chair in front of a window with the shade pulled down and back to the radio where he sat. "I like the way the muscles in your calves tighten up and stand out. Baby, you sure have long legs. You could've been a dancer. Gone to Broadway. Joined the Rockettes."

"Oh, Bob, you think I'm still pretty?"

"I sure do, and if I didn't have this damned headache I'd show you."

Clarice was distraught. It was time to call another meeting and see if the other women had similar problems.

"George hasn't said anything or made any innuendos about the lack of sex. It's like it doesn't matter that much to him. I got worried, so last night I put on the slinkiest lingerie in my dresser drawer and paraded around the living room while he read the paper." She paused.

"Go on, Summer. What happened?"

"Nothing."

"Nothing happened? Nothing at all?"

"No. He kept reading the paper. Once he got up and changed the radio station and glanced at me. I was making the most seductive pose I could. I didn't have all the buttons fastened. Hell, hardly any buttons fastened. I was falling out the top and had one leg wrapped around the umbrella stand. He walked into the bedroom. When he came out, I lay on my stomach on the sofa, hugging a pillow and showing a little cheek. He dropped a quilt over me, saying I looked cold. He then went back to reading the paper." She looked around the room. "I don't think Georgie thinks I'm sexy anymore." Summer Satterfield sat down and starting crying. Marge handed her a handkerchief and patted her on the back.

Betty Baker raised her hand. "My John still loves me. We haven't had any sex and he's quit asking, but he still opens the car door for me and tells me I'm pretty, even when I'm not."

"But how do you know for sure?"

"Uh . . . I don't have any sworn statements. No court rulings. Nothing to back up what I believe but My John. I just know it, and I vote we stop this masquerade and get back to normalcy."

"Anyone else?"

Boyd's girlfriend stood beside her chair. "It's not working anymore."

"What's not working?"

"The banana thing. It doesn't matter what I do to the banana, Boyd could care less. Last night he got up from the porch swing and went inside the house for a moment. When he came back he had a wash rag. He handed it to me and said I had banana all over my face. I'm afraid I've lost control of the situation."

"Ophelia, have you any comments?"

"Just that the powdered rhino horn doesn't seem to work. I've given it to him in his oatmeal, dusted it over his eggs, and dissolved it in his orange juice. Monday night I gave it one last effort. I mixed it with some ointment he uses on cow udders. I waited until he was good and asleep, then I dipped my fingers into the doctored ointment and reached under the covers."

"Uh . . . Ophelia, you don't have to give us the minutiae."

"No, I want to hear it."

"Me too."

"Oh, all right. Ophelia, what did you do when you reached under the covers?"

"Well, he was snoring to beat sixty. So I touched his leg, then walked my fingertips up to, and inside, his shorts."

"I can't listen anymore."

"Me neither. That's too smutty for me."

Boyd's girlfriend spoke up, "Go on. What happened next?"

"Okay, Ophelia. Skip the vulgar stuff. What was the outcome?"

"Nothing. I smeared it on from top to bottom and nothing happened."

"How long did you wait?"

I don't know. I lay there waiting with my hand wrapped around him and fell asleep. The next morning, he was up, showered, and out the door before I even got up."

CHAPTER 30—ADELLE'S REVENGE

The new appliances arrived and Claude's first job was to take out the old cabinetry and old appliances to make way for the new. It took him two days to remove everything and to clean up his mess. With the new appliances properly hooked up and where Adelle wanted them, he could start to measure and build her new cabinets.

Claude set up his sawhorses outside Adelle's kitchen door. He'd measure the space and proceed to the back yard to cut the needed piece of lumber. Adelle wanted her cabinets made of maple because the wood was slick to the touch and wouldn't easily dent if a plate was dropped while being put away. But she wanted her cabinet doors to be a golden oak with glass inserts. They were a labor intensive set of cabinets, using only the best of materials.

The sawmill in Moccasin Gap could produce any kind of lumber needed and, after the first month, quit producing the basic two-by-fours and two-by-sixes needed for the ball field. Now, they were back to a wider repertoire including trim and doors. With the addition of Adelle's kitchen, Claude asked for trim in oak. He had to cut, miter, and join the pieces to strict tolerances. Claude was a perfectionist and Adelle appreciated quality craftsmanship.

The first day of construction Adelle fixed Claude lunch. "Claude, what do you think about this old house?"

"I think it's a fine example of a large farmhouse where functionality plays a more important role than aesthetics."

"My grandfather loved it. He said it was a lot like him: not very modern but well put together."

"I also think your grandfather liked it because it came with its own thermal spring."

"Yes, that too." Adelle poured more iced tea. "It's drafty in winter and not all the chimneys draw well. There's four bedrooms upstairs—each with its own fireplace—but only two of them will keep a fire going. I asked Emmett if he would look at them, but he told me his expertise did not extend to things accomplished with sweat."

"I'll look at them before I finish. They're probably clogged with built-up creosote. If that's the case, you'll have to have them professionally cleaned or you could burn the place down."

"And the chains on the dumb waiters need replacing. The cook never could get anything delivered from the kitchen. And some of the windows don't open. During the summer I need all the windows open to let the breeze in. I could go on."

"You might find it more economical to find a boyfriend with home repair skills."

"No. From now on it's all for love. I'll pay someone like you to do the work and reserve my affection for someone who feeds my passion."

"But look how much better off you'd be if that someone had both skills."

"That person would be a treasure indeed."

The next day Claude did not bring his lunch pail. He expected Adelle to tell him how clean her kitchen looked with the old cabinets removed and to reward his hard work with more of her cooking magic. He was mistaken.

At eleven-thirty that morning, Emmett came through the door without knocking. He gave a close scrutinizing look at Claude's dismantling and went looking for Adelle. A few minutes later, they were in Emmett's car heading to town. Claude continued to work, then took a break and decided to help himself to whatever was in her new refrigerator. When he finished that evening, she had not returned, so he turned off the lights, locked both doors, and went home.

The next day Claude brought his lunch pail. It was a good thing because Adelle prepared a meal for Emmett. They ate in the garden, then changed clothes and got into the tub of hot water. Claude watched through the kitchen windows as he worked. He was now putting up the basic structure. Occasionally he glanced out the window to see what they were doing. When he did this, sometimes his hammer's head slapped the nail at an angle and slipping off the nail head dented the wood. Each time this happened he had to stop and douse the dent with water, He then set a hot poker on a wet towel sitting on the soaked dent. Soon, the wood swelled and the dent miraculously disappeared. But the problem causing the dent in the first place continued.

Adelle had a wrought iron table within their reach, holding a pitcher of iced tea and another of iced water. They soaked in the tub, drank liberal quantities of the cool liquids, and talked quietly about things Claude could not hear.

Adelle was the most exciting woman Claude had ever met and she seemed oblivious to his charm. He became infatuated with her and her ability to throttle his magnetism.

It was Friday and Claude stopped to admire his work. When he finished that afternoon he would be almost finished with the construction. He figured Monday he'd start staining and adding the first of several coats of shellac. On Friday he could add the glass inserts and be finished.

"Claude, they're looking so good. Let me fix you lunch to show my appreciation."

"Appreciation accepted."

Thirty minutes later, they dipped spoons in bowls of wild mushroom soup and ate corned beef and sauerkraut sandwiches. Adelle also fixed iced tea to which she had added pureed fruit.

"Adelle, what do you see in Emmett?"

"Emmett doesn't hide anything from you. What you see is what you get. No surprises. He's well educated. He's striving to better himself. He reads, likes to travel, and sees things in the big picture. But he lacks spontaneity, creativity, and depth of character. And he's miserly with his money and affection. However, when I weigh his good points counterbalanced with his bad, I find he definitely tips the scale to the positive side. He's asked me to marry him." Adelle gave a close look at Claude. "Do you think I should accept?"

"Adelle, he only wants your money so he can run for office."

"Yes, I know. He told me that up front."

"But you told me, 'From now on it's all for love.' You said you reserved your affection for someone who could feed your passion. Does he do that?"

"Claude, you . . . did I say that?"

"You did, and I was impressed."

"You're right. I need to decide if Emmett can stimulate me emotionally. I can't jump into matrimony until I have that assurance. Thank you, Claude, for helping me to see my future."

"And if he comes up short, would there be an opportunity for another knight to step forward and, with his lance tilted in your direction, ask to carry your colors?"

"What a lovely thing to say. Have you read anything by Sir Walter Scott—other than Ivanhoe?"

"No. But I've read everything written by Alexandre Dumas."

CHAPTER 31—DINNER AT THE RITZ

"Claude, I need to see you."

"Hello, Meredith. I've been kind of busy. My brother and I have had to change directions with our business and it's taken all my time to get things going."

"So, can we have dinner tonight?"

"Meredith, are you sure? I'm twenty-five years older than you."

"It's only a number, Claude. What matters is how we feel toward each other. And I feel wonderful when I'm around you. I've made reservations at the Ritz for tonight at seven. Can I pick you up? Dad's bought me a new car and I want to show it off."

"Okay, you know where the Townsend Boarding House is located?"

"Yes."

"Pick me up at six, I'll be standing out front and we'll drive around town first."

Adelle and Emmett also had made plans to eat at the Ritz Bistro. When they arrived, they were seated at a table close to the piano, completely across the room from where Claude and Meredith were placed. Emmett pulled out Adelle's chair. He removed his jacket and placed it on his chair back. A handsome, middle-aged woman played a nocturne by Chopin.

"We need another quality restaurant. I detest Bill Potter, and every time I come in here I feel like I'm feeding money to a huge rat. I think his food is over-priced, and this wine list is unbelievable. I can't believe a bottle of wine is worth ten dollars."

"Emmett, most of the bottles are less than five dollars and the house wines—the ones you buy—are half that. And his prices are market-driven. If his patrons won't pay the price, Mr. Potter will be forced to lower them or carry a larger assortment of cheaper varietals."

"Well, what do you think of a steak for seven dollars? Is that not out of sight?"

"No. If you'll notice, the menu says the meat is USDA Prime. That's the most expensive grade. If he used USDA Choice, that seven-dollar steak would be in the three-fifty to four dollar price range. And USDA Good, the grade most places use, would be even less. You get what you pay for. USDA Prime is as good as it gets.

"And, besides that, have you forgotten the chef? Bill's hired a world-class chef. Part of the cost has to cover his salary. And then there's all this atmosphere. I'd also like to see another quality restaurant, but they better not take this one away."

Across the room, Meredith looked into the clear, steel-gray eyes of her date. "I told my father about you. He said you were too old."

"I agree."

"He bought me the car as a bribe."

"Maybe, he'll send you away to an art institute for painting lessons."

"You think a woman's heart can so easily be bought?"

"No, but why not take advantage of the situation?"

"I want it all, not bits and pieces. He can afford to send me for lessons and I could drag you along as well. With art occupying my days and you for my nights, I'd be in heaven."

"Meredith, you'll find someone who shares your enthusiasm for painting and who's closer to your age. While you might be caught up in the moment with me right now, it won't be like that in ten years. Could you have a passionate kiss with someone wearing false teeth?"

"I don't want to hear it. Let's order and enjoy being together right now."

At the table by the piano, Adelle waited while Emmett, with an air of hauteur, looked through the wine list.

"I can never decide which wine to order."

"Emmett, you need to order a wine that will complement your entrée."

"I haven't even looked at that menu yet."

"Narrow it down. Do you plan on ordering something heavy like a steak, prime rib, or pasta? If you are, order a full-bodied red. On the other hand, if you plan on ordering something light like fish or chicken, then order a white. Pork usually requires a white. Sweet or fortified wines come after dinner."

Emmett looked up from the wine list. "Adelle, here is a new rule for you. Don't try to show up your date. You could get left at the table."

"I wasn't trying to show you up. You said you had a difficult time deciding on a wine so I thought I'd give you some information. Emmett, do you think women are subservient to men?"

"No, I don't. But I don't want one to think she's smarter than me either."

"And what if she is?"

"Is what?"

"Smarter than you."

"It won't happen."

"You mean, there are no women smarter than you?"

"There are no women smarter than me who I would consider taking anywhere."

"Then you think I am less smart than you?"

"I didn't say that."

"And, then syllogistically, I must also be less smart than those people smarter than you.

Let me see. There are quite a few people in that category. There's Michael Jellico and Bill Potter, and even that stupid sheriff had you buffaloed. It's a wonder I can come in from the rain."

Adelle took the napkin from her lap, placed it on the table, and headed for the door. Emmett's jaw dropped. He jumped from his chair and followed Adelle, asking her to come back. Not to embarrass him in public. The *maitre d'* stepped forward and whispered something in Adelle's ear. She wheeled and went into the women's powder room, leaving a bewildered Emmett not knowing what to do.

"What'd you say to her?"

"I said I'd call her a taxi and she could wait in the ladies' room."

"She's no business of yours."

"Mr. Irving, I've been told if you cause the least bit of trouble, to escort you to the door and kick your scrawny ass to the sidewalk."

"Well, I never."

"And you never will again, either."

"Never what?"

"Be allowed to eat in the Bistro or to attend any gala in the Ballroom." With that he snapped his fingers and Percy, from the lounge, leaped over the bar and, in three giant strides, stood next to his boss. "Percy, I have asked Mr. Irving to leave. Please see that he gets his coat and help him to the front door."

"With pleasure."

"Get your hands off me."

"Now, get along Mr. Irving. Mind the step. Oh, I'm sorry, Mr. Irving. Here, let me help you up. Good Lord, Mr. Irving can you not get your footing? Oh hell, now I've stepped on your pant's leg. I'll just grab your belt here and help you up. Stewart, would you get Mr. Irving's coat while I hold him up? He's having the devil of a time standing. See there, he did it again."

"I'll talk to Bill about you. I'll have your job, buster."

"Please do, Mr. Irving. Mr. Potter will probably give me a pay raise. Stewart, get the door. It's taking both of my hands to keep Mr. Irving from slipping to the floor. Oh, man, see what I mean?"

"I'll see you in court."

"That might be interesting. I think you ought to give it a try. We have Mr. Jellico on retainer."

CHAPTER 32—MEREDITH ASSERTS

On Monday, Claude started staining. He spent two hours meticulously cleaning away bits of sawdust and specks of dried wood putty. His finish nails had been driven just below the wood surface and covered with a tiny amount of stainable wood putty. When he had finished sanding last Friday no nails showed.

The first coat of stain was applied over a small section and timed before being wiped dry with a soft cloth. Adelle watched from her chair.

"Adelle, we can make it darker but not lighter without sanding into the wood. If we make it too light the grain of the wood won't stand out. Too dark and we lose the golden glow. How does this look?"

"Claude, your work is wonderful. I do think it ought to be a little darker, though."

"How's this?"

"I think you've got it. I may never want to move."

"Aren't you going to move to Little Rock, if Emmett gets elected to the House of Representatives or the Governorship?"

"Don't talk of that man." There was a knock on the door. Adelle opened to a hand extending a big vase of flowers.

"These are for a Miss Adelle Peterson."

"I'm Adelle Peterson. Thank you so much."

Back at the kitchen table, she set the vase down and plucked out a small envelope. "They're from Emmett. Says he's sorry for stepping on my toes."

Fifteen minutes later, there's another knock on the door and another vase of flowers from Emmett. Then in another ten minutes, there's another knock on the door. Adelle yanked open the door. Meredith stood on her porch.

"I came to see if I could take your carpenter to lunch."

"Hello, I'm Adelle Peterson." Adelle held out her hand.

"Yes. I've seen your picture in the paper. I'm Meredith Creighton—Claude's girlfriend."

"Come in, Miss Creighton."

"Wow, Claude, those cabinets look like they should be entered in a wood-working competition." Meredith walked over to Claude and, standing on her tip-toes, kissed him on the cheek.

"Its twelve o'clock. Can you break for lunch?"

"I need to put on a little more stain, then I'll have an hour or so while it dries."

Meredith turned to Adelle. "Isn't he something?"

"Yes, I believe he is."

Adelle's telephone rang and she excused herself to go answer it in the front room. "Yes, I got the flowers. Yes, both vases. A little extravagant for someone who only spends money for show." Adelle sat in a chair.

"I'm sorry about last night, Adelle. I'd like to talk to you. I didn't express my true feelings or my real opinion of the relationship between men and women. If you would see me again I promise to behave like a true gentleman. I thought I'd cook for you. We could eat on the balcony. My apartment is on the second floor and I have a good view of City Park. What do you say?"

"I don't know, Emmett. Just a second." Adelle got up from the chair and stole a look into her kitchen. Meredith had removed her shoes and now faced Claude while standing on his shoes in her stockings. Claude was looking over Meredith's shoulder and reaching around her waist, applying stain. She had both arms around his neck and her body pressed against his. It looked like she was kissing, or nibbling, on his neck. Adelle went back to the telephone. "So you live in that brownstone across the street from the park?"

"Yes . . . I—"

"I had no idea you were so close. How about I walk over around five? Will that give you enough time to do your cooking?"

"I think so."

"Okay. I'll see you then, but I'm warning you, mister. You better be on your best behavior."

Meredith parked her new car in the small paved parking lot next to the entrance to City Park and, from its trunk, retrieved a wicker basket of food and a thermos of iced tea. She let Claude carry the food. As they walked to one of the wrought iron tables beside a pool of calm water, she reached for his hand and interlaced her fingers with his.

"Claude, I'm so glad to be with you today."

"It was an easy decision. I had to choose between a baloney sandwich on the one hand and, on the other, a fine meal of fried chicken in a flower garden with a beautiful woman. You won hands down. In fact, the baloney sandwich was so far behind it didn't even place second."

"No? What placed second?"

"That would be me watching you eat the fried chicken."

"And, third?"

"Me watching you eat the baloney sandwich."

"Claude Calhoun, you are too much. When I'm with you, I feel like everything is about me. But I want to know about you. What do you like? Where have you been? What have you done?"

"I like all things beautiful. I've never been out of northern Arkansas. And I haven't done a tenth of what I've dreamed."

"More. I want more."

"I read. I become one with the character in the story. I live his life, in his world, and help him solve his problems. I can do many things because I've read about them and, with my eyes closed, have almost achieved out-of-body experiences. I feel I could actually shoot a long-bow, argue with Socrates, drive a chariot, journey to the center of the earth, even vie with Mr. Darcy for Elizabeth Bennett's hand. Books give me a larger world in which to operate. But that doesn't mean that someday I won't set the book down and actually do what I've been reading about. My new business might be the steed I ride through the periphery of my desire."

"Claude, I love listening to you talk."

That afternoon Adelle, watched Claude transform her cabinets into something showcased in a magazine. She sensed that, when he ran his hand along the length of the wood, he was caressing it, loving it.

And the cabinets, in return, glowed warm and magnificent. Claude was the man. But, he was not yet her man.

By four-thirty she was dressed and ready to head to Emmett's. She anticipated this to be Emmett's last stand. When she arrived at his apartment he told her she might need to keep on her coat. He then kissed her awkwardly and ushered her past his tawdry furnishings to the balcony. There was a small table with two chairs on one end, and an upside-down milk crate holding a small grill on the other.

"I couldn't figure a way to cook vegetables on the grill, so I put on two baked potatoes."

Adelle pulled her coat tight. "That'll be fine, Emmett. What else is under the lid?"

"Two steaks."

"What cut of steak?"

"I'm sorry, I don't know one from another. At the restaurant, I go strictly by price. So I went to the butcher and asked for two of his best steaks. I think you'll like it. But I had the fire up too hot at first and now it's taking a long time for the potatoes."

"Do you have any bread? A salad maybe?"

"No."

"What do you have to drink?"

"I've got sodas, orange juice, and water."

"I'll take a soda."

"They're in the refrigerator."

Adelle waited a moment then said, "No, don't bother. I can find the refrigerator."

In a few minutes, Adelle was sitting in one of the chairs looking out over City Park. "You don't have much in your refrigerator. Do you eat at home often?"

"No."

"So, Emmett, how differently do you see the role of women versus the role of men?"

"Uh . . . women are different than men. They . . . uh, have different requirements. I've noticed they eat smaller quantities of food and sleep shorter periods of time. Physically, they're usually shorter, not quite as strong, not all that interested in things outside their kitchen, and usually needing one thing or another."

"I see. So what good are we?"

"Our species would die out if it weren't for women replenishing the stock. And, usually, men don't do so good around the house. I guess you've noticed, things are strewn throughout the apartment. Maybe even noticed the stove doesn't work."

"It doesn't work?"

"I can't get it to come on. You didn't go into the bathroom, did you?"

"I did, but I wish I hadn't."

"I'm sorry about that. I was going to clean it, but don't have a mop or any cleaning supplies."

"Emmett, let me look at the food." Adelle walked over to the grill and raised the cover. With the one implement available, she poked first at the steaks and then the potatoes. She then lowered the cover and turned to Emmett. "I don't see any salt or pepper."

"I couldn't find any."

"Emmett, you skimped on the charcoal. You tried to cook using lighter fluid to keep the fire going. Now, one steak is burnt on the outside, and both are raw on the inside. You didn't add any seasoning and the potatoes, over that paltry fire, will never finish cooking. The charcoal will burn down to nothing first. Let's go to the Ritz and have the meal we should have had last night."

"I can't."

"What do you mean you can't?"

"The *maitre d'* said I wasn't welcome any more, and I'm not allowed to go to any of the performances at the ballroom either."

"Emmett, I have a new rule for you . . . you're . . . you're toast."

CHAPTER 33—IN BED WITH BEAR

It was two o'clock on a cold afternoon in late November when Horace Honeycut and his helpers knocked on Chester's door. Snow had fallen earlier in the week and the deeper drifts had not completely melted. Ducks and geese from Canada had long passed overhead on their journey to warmer latitudes and animals that hibernate were deep in their winter homes waiting for warmer times.

Horace couldn't get anything out of Charley, but Tarleton said there was only one other trail and he knew where it was. So they ran out the door and followed a barefoot little boy who had already spent his reward money a dozen times.

Fifty feet up the trail, Tarleton started hopping on one foot and yelling mild obscenities.

Honeycut caught up with Tarleton, "What's the matter, boy?"

Tarleton sat down, holding one of his feet. "Tacks. He's scattered tacks on the trail."

Cameron reached in his pocket and curled his hand around a gun. Honeycut hadn't said anything about a gun, so he thought it might be good insurance. Anyway, Honeycut said the broad would pay whether Wainwright was dead or alive. He might be easier to handle toted over a shoulder with a .45 slug in his back.

"Boy, you hobble back to that cabin. Ask the girl if she'll clean your wound with alcohol. We'll figure some way to haul you back after we catch him."

"Thank you, sir. That's my clutching foot."

"You thinking about driving my truck before giving it back?"

"Uh . . . no sir. Not unless it's absolutely necessary."

"John, got your camera? You and Cameron follow me. We need to catch Wainwright before dark."

"Honeycut, there he is." John was pointing his finger through the trees to an open spot. "He's watching us." John raised his camera.

Horace looked in the direction the finger had pointed. Cameron yelled, "Let's get him."

Horace looked at the hulk he had brought in case there might be trouble. "Hold on, Cameron. He didn't do nothing to be running. Let's hold up a white flag and see if he'll parley."

Cameron didn't listen. This was the first chance he'd had to put the hurt on someone without the possibility of spending a night in jail. He was up the trail before Honeycut had finished talking, but he was big and he was slow. John easily overtook him and John was carrying a cumbersome camera.

A hundred yards along the trail, John's knee broke a slender strand of thread stretched across the narrow trail and stepped in a loop of rope on the ground. A pin attached to the string was pulled out of a catch and a heavy log fell from its precarious perch. A rope tied around its center rose from the log up sixty feet into the tree and over a stout branch. When the log slid down a steep embankment in a spade-dug chute, John shot up high into the tree, the other end of the rope tight around his ankle. He continued higher and higher in the tree as the log descended. The tree towered over the path, proudly holding the invader sixty feet in the air, his arms flailing wildly.

"Help. Someone, get me down."

Cameron was first on the scene but didn't want to stop. Besides, John was too far off the ground to suit Cameron. He kept going after the quarry, now wary of the backwoods savvy of the New York cop. "Hold on, John, Honeycut's right behind me." He continued a few more yards. "I think I see him. He's laughing at us."

"Cameron, come back here. I'm getting dizzy."

Horace came upon John who was now crying. "Damnit Honeycut, get me down. All the blood's rushed to my head. I think I'm going to faint."

"My God. How'd you get way up there? You still got the camera?"

"Yeah, its on a strap over my shoulder. I think I got his picture. I don't know how I got up here, but I can tell you what I'm going to do when I get down."

"Now, John, don't be hasty. Get a good hold on the camera and keep it close to your body. If you fall, try and not damage it. We'll need that picture. I'll figure some way to get you down."

Horace followed the rope down the chute to the log. After he untied the rope, he let it pull him back up the chute as it lowered John to the ground. It took him almost fifteen minutes to get a whimpering John back to earth. On the ground, John was shaking. "Damn you, Honeycut. Here's your camera. I'm going back."

Cameron yelled back over his shoulder. "I got him. He's right here in front of me." Cameron huffed and puffed. "Damnit, Wainwright. Stop right there. We ain't going to hurt you."

Cameron hadn't noticed that the trail had gradually ascended for the last two hundred yards. Now there was a steep ravine to his right. To his left were tall trees and thick underbrush. One large branch was pulled back and held in place with the slimmest of contrivances. Cameron tripped on a stick stuck in the soil, dislodging the brace holding back the branch. Now free, it snapped back into place, hitting Cameron in the chest and knocking him over the edge of the path. He tumbled down the precipitous ravine, picking up speed and slamming against large rocks as he sailed by. At the bottom, he caromed off the base of a large tree and landed unconscious in a shallow cave.

Horace came to the place where the branch had knocked Cameron off the trail. Not seeing anything unusual, he continued on. "Cameron . . . Cameron. Where are you?"

Horace stopped and listened. This time of year it got dark early. He didn't want to be in the woods after dark. He had his picture . . . at least, he thought he had his picture. He needed to round up his helpers and head back to town. He'd come back tomorrow.

"Cameron. Come on back. It'll be dark in an hour. Let's give it another go tomorrow. Cameron . . . Cameron, can you hear me? I'm going back to the cabin and then back to the boy's home. Cameron, come on, let's go."

Back at Chester's cabin, Horace and a shaken John picked up Tarleton. He said to Chester, "If you can put Cameron up for the night I'll give you five dollars. I'll be back in the morning and start again." He walked to the door. "Now, I don't want to get you alarmed or anything. The man ain't done nothing wrong. He's from New York City and he's got some friends looking for him. They're the ones offering the big reward. Looks like that money is going to the boy here. If he comes in wanting something to eat tell him we don't mean him no harm. You might want to keep Cameron away from him though. Cameron's the mean one, not your Tom."

With that said, Honeycut picked up Tarleton and stuck him on his shoulders. "Boy, your mommy's going to have a fit when she finds out you got hurt. That tack went into your foot up to its head. Does it hurt much?"

"Naw. It was him, wasn't it?"

Horace headed out the door. "I think so, but I don't know how a New Yorker could have planted all those traps."

"Demas did it. People around here think he's slow, but he's not. He's plenty smart."

"Is Demas that kid about your age, hiding behind the girl?"

"Yep. He's probably got so many traps laid he's forgotten where half are hid. If it's all right with you I'll stay at the cabin tomorrow and try to get some information out of him. We're good friends."

"He might not be such a good friend now that you squealed on Wainwright."

"Then I may have to buy him something outta my reward money."

After they returned and let his mother look at Tarleton's foot, Horace said he needed the keys to his truck so they could go into Carthage for the night.

"Boy, we'll be back in the morning. I'll give you back the keys tomorrow."

"What can you give me to hold, so I'll know you'll be back?"

"Cameron is still out there. I've got to come back." He looked at the boy with his hands folded across his chest. "All I got's my wallet and this camera."

Tarleton's face lit up, "I could drive you into town and come back and pick you up tomorrow morning."

"Boy, how old are you?"

"Ten."

"In this state, you're not allowed to drive till you're sixteen. Let me have the roll of film and you can keep the camera, the tripod, and both our wallets. I think I got fifty dollars in mine. You take that or we stay the night."

Tarleton's mother said, "Tarleton, give him his keys. I'm getting tired of listening to you fooling with him."

CHAPTER 33—THANKSGIVING IN APPALACHIA

As the Pike Brothers' Floating Store crept upstream against the current, Faye had time to reflect. She had been hunting for W.W. for over two months. Autumn had turned to winter. Snow fell. People wore heavy coats, caps with earmuffs, and mufflers. Christmas was on the horizon. And, before Bear made the mention about the little boy's dog, she had almost given up. But now, she was heading to him. Faye would gather him in her arms and make his hurt go away.

Katy and Bear had unpleasant things to say about the weather, and the wind, and the dining arrangements, and the food prepared—but not Faye. She had a smile on her face and a warm feeling in her heart.

Bear still jumped overboard every morning to bathe, but he couldn't talk Katy into joining him, and his visits to the water had become brief. He jumped in, made a few off-color remarks, quickly shampooed his hair and scrubbed with soap, and then he yelled for Jim to pull him back. Afterwards he sat with his fellow passengers on deck around the tent heater and shivered. He said it was mind over matter but couldn't convince anyone to join him for a daily bath.

On Thanksgiving day they pulled up to Chester's dock. Faye was the first one off. She ran to the little shack and knocked on the door.

"Where is he? Where's W.W?"

Charley said, "Come in out of the cold. We don't know. And that big man didn't show up last night either."

"What big man?"

The rest of the group clamored at the door to get inside. Soon everyone huddled with their backsides encircling the wood-burning heater.

"Yesterday Tarleton sold him out. He brought that newspaper fella from Carthage and two others down the east trail. Tom heard the warning signal and left up the west trail. Demas was working the traps and Pa was upstream in the boat. So, after asking me where he was,

139

Tarleton said he knew of the other trail and they high-tailed it. In a little while Tarleton hobbled back with a tack in his foot, then just before dark the man with the camera came in saying he was through. He was followed by that newspaper fella who said the big guy was lost and he'd pay us five dollars if we gave him shelter if he showed up. But he didn't. And we ain't seen Tom either."

"And this Tom. He's the one who's teaching you to read and write?"

"Yes, ma'am."

"And he's the one who named the dog, Radix?"

"Yes, ma'am."

"Then, your Tom and my W.W. are the same man. You've got to help me find him. We were going to get married before he fell out of that train and landed in the river."

"Tom don't know who he is or where he come from."

Faye sat down and Charley started to make coffee. Jim Pike said, "Charley, today's Thanksgiving. Were you planning on a special meal for the boys?"

"Yeah, but we ain't got much."

"I got a whole store tied up at your dock. If you'll let us we'll haul in enough to do it up right."

Katy said, "And I'll help cook."

"Kate, I've heard about your cooking. You better be a cook's helper," said Bear.

"What's that supposed to mean?"

"Did you once try to cook something for a police officer?"

"Yes, the one whose windshield and driver's side window got hit by a ricocheting bullet."

"He's a regular customer of mine. He told me about this good-looking woman who couldn't toast bread. After talking with him for a few minutes, I realized he was talking about you. And on this trip all you and your sister have been able to do was open a few cans of tuna fish."

"Well, buster, no desperate woman thing for you."

"Now, Kate, it doesn't mean that much to me. I don't care that you can't cook. I like the other things you can do."

"Like what?"

"I'll tell you when we're to ourselves."

"Okay. I never pretended to be a cook anyway."

Cameron gradually came back to life with a large knot over his right ear. He still saw stars when a small amount of daylight wandered into the recesses of the cave. There was a stench so bad he had trouble breathing. And, a heavy branch lay on top, pinning him down. Cameron turned over. When he did he looked nose to nose into the face of a hibernating black bear. Cameron slowly moved his hand to his pocket for the gun. It wasn't there.

The bear's eyes followed his hand as it came out of his pocket. Hell, the bear's awake. But, thank God, not fully awake. He needed to get out of there fast. He'd heard stories of bears rousing themselves out of hibernation. He needed to slip out from under the bear's arm, roll to the opening, and then run. But the more he tried to lift the arm, the more the bear pushed down. Maybe, if he lay still, the bear might revert back into a deeper state of hibernation and then he'd leave.

CHAPTER 34—THANKSGIVING IN DANCING DEER

In Dancing Deer, eleven families, all the members of the city council—except Bill Potter—stood behind a large serving line in the high school gymnasium. The children of the families refilled drinks, cleaned tables, and served pumpkin and pecan pie.

Ophelia Obadiah asked, "So where's Bill?" She filled people's bowls with pinto beans as they passed in front with empty trays.

Clarice answered, "He and Harriet are still on their honeymoon. There's a bulletin board at the Ritz with postcards and pictures they've sent. I think they're now at Yellowstone National Park and Bill broke his leg."

"Running with wolves?"

"No, learning to ski. On the card, Harriet said he didn't mind. He's been staying in the lodge in front of a roaring fire doctored up on liquor. She says he's now an expert on all drinks containing coconut, or butter, or rum, or heated up."

"When will they come back?"

"In time for Christmas. This'll be their first Christmas as a family and they want to celebrate it with Rose and her family."

"It's a shame they couldn't be here to see what his betting with our husbands has accomplished."

Johnston Baker carved on a roasted turkey. "Yeah, we're gonna feed over three hundred people today, but not all of them would have gone without a decent dinner."

"I think it's wonderful. A lot of Dancing Deer citizens turned out to eat with those less fortunate. They brought their own covered dishes and pitchers of tea. I'll bet half of the people are here for the fellowship." Summer Satterfield used a gigantic spoon to scoop mounds of mashed potatoes.

George Satterfield was the next in the serving line. It was his duty to ladle on brown gravy. "I'm glad several of our members are also on the school board. Without the school buses, we wouldn't have been able to bring in the people from Skunk Hollow or Cakebread. We quite possibly could have prepared a meal for the homeless and not found any homeless to give it to. Well, we do have Cody. Where is he anyway?"

Clarice poured iced tea. " He's in the back washing dishes. It's a shame most of these people can't vote in our town elections."

Bob wrapped forks, spoons, and knives in napkins. "Clarice has decided to run against me for mayor in the next election. We're trying to keep it in the family. Sort of like a dynasty thing."

"That's funny."

"Yeah, we'll have you stand on stumps in front of the courthouse and debate."

"Well, if Mona wants my seat on the city council, she can have it."

"You say that now, Jerry, but when it comes time to run again you'll want Mona in your camp bringing all her friends to the voting booths. I'll bet most of the people voting are women."

Mayor Bob said, "If that's truly the case, I've got my hands full against Clarice."

At the Creighton house, Mr. and Mrs. Creighton tried their best to entertain their daughter's new boyfriend.

"So tell me, Claude, where have you been this last year? Meredith says you've just returned to start working with your brother."

"Mr. Creighton . . ."

"Call me Carl. After all, I am younger than you."

"All right, Carl. I was managing an investment for a group of ladies in Fort Smith. They paid me handsomely so when Rupert started his construction business, I came back to help him and paid for a half interest in the company."

"Claude, would that investment in Fort Smith be The Painted Lady."

"Uh . . . yes sir. You've heard of The Painted Lady?"

"I carry hefty insurance policies because of the nature of my inventory. The insurance company I use has a branch office in Fort Smith. Their investigators gave me all the information I needed. Claude, we don't have any painted ladies in Dancing Deer. What are you going to do if this new construction venture doesn't work out?"

Meredith butted in, "Claude, what is a painted lady?"

"A painted lady is a . . . a house . . . uh, a house that is Victorian in design. They're usually painted in pastel colors with white picket fences."

"And you managed this house?"

Claude stole a quick glance at Mr. Creighton. He had a satisfied grin on his face. "I didn't manage what went on in the house. I was the building's caretaker. In return for providing me a room and a hefty salary, I did all of the maintenance. I also protected the house's employees. They were all women."

Mrs. Creighton said, "Were these ladies operating a quilting club?"

"Uh, no . . . more like a social club. They had a Victrola with hundreds of recorded disks. I think they'd purchased one of those new phonographs when I left but it hadn't arrived. It would play seventy-eights."

"A garden club then?"

"No, they were more into entertaining."

Mrs. Creighton was flustered. "So, how do they make their money?"

"They charged for providing the entertainment."

"Like a show?"

"Yes, I think 'show' might be a good term, if you mean providing a scenario where the participants playact their parts using fictitious names and silly costumes. 'Farce' might also be a good descriptive term."

Meredith said, "We have the Ritz Grand Ballroom here. They put on shows. They also have musicians, vaudeville acts, and magicians. I understand there was even a boxing match while I was away at school."

Claude was sweating when Polly, the cook, entered the room and said the meal was ready. Polly busied herself making sure each person had his beverage of choice and access to all of her dishes. Mr. Creighton stood at the head of the table and, after he blessed the food, proceeded to carve the turkey.

"Claude, have you ever been married?"

"No, sir."

"You might not remember me, but I was in seventh grade when you dropped out during your eighth. I don't remember you as being the sophisticated man I now see, and I think we all remember the night you danced with that newspaper lady. I thought a woman's influence might have made the difference."

"I've had dance lessons."

"So, besides your carpentry skills and your dancing ability, everything else is self-taught."

"Yes, sir, all from books."

"Very honorable. Do you know anything about jewelry?"

"I know how to use a loop to look for inclusions in a diamond. I can tell the difference between gold and gold-plated, and I can make crystal sing."

Mrs. Creighton beamed. "You must show us how crystal sings."

"I'd love to." Claude picked up his water goblet and thumped it with his fingernail. He held it up to his ear and then peered through it at the overhead light. He said, "I think this might be Czechoslovakian." Then he dipped his finger in the water and ran it slowly around the rim of the glass. The goblet let out a low melodious rumble. "The pitch would be higher with less water. The sound waves travel slower through a liquid. Conversely, with more water, the sound would be lower. With a set of eight, and each with the amount of water necessary to emit the pitch of a note on the harmonic scale, a skillful person could play a tune."

"Oh, that's wonderful." Mrs. Creighton clapped her hands. "Did you know that, Carl?"

"Yes, honey. You forget I sell the stuff. It's my business to know everything about it. Sometimes a little knowledge like that makes the difference in a customer buying or just looking."

"Polly, do we have eight extra goblets?"

Polly stood off to one side. She was waiting for praise for her cooking. "Yes, ma'am."

146

"Then, after we eat, bring them into the family room with a pitcher of water. Meredith's going to talk Claude into playing Christmas songs."

Meredith looked in Claude's direction and winked.

"Now, don't get your hopes up, Emmett. I've decided not to marry you, but I still think of you as a friend and I wouldn't want a friend to be alone on Thanksgiving. So if you'd like to enjoy a fine meal in my new kitchen, then come over around eleven."

"Thanks, Adelle, I'll be there."

Adelle would have asked Claude but found out at the beauty salon that Meredith had already invited him to her house.

"Gena, I'd like something outlandish. I'd like to take ten years off with a new hairdo. Have you got any suggestions?"

"Miss Peterson, your hair is beautiful as it is. I have people in all the time asking me if I can color their hair a golden brown. Sometimes they call it dark blond or strawberry blond but it's the color of your hair they're describing. We might try a new style though. Why don't you look through the movie-star magazines? If you see something you like, I'll do my best to duplicate it."

Adelle grabbed one of the magazines as she waited her turn for the chair and hungrily looked for a new, captivating style.

"Miss Peterson, I've heard Claude Calhoun is building you new kitchen cabinets."

"Yes, and they are magnificent. The man has a taste for style. I gave him full freedom on their design. I couldn't be happier."

"My nephew is also a carpenter. I asked him to do some work for me and he said the Calhouns have a lock on all the lumber. When Claude came back, he and Rupert cornered the market and now they have all the business in town. The other carpenters are having to work for the Calhoun Construction Company just to feed their families. I think it's outrageous. And now I understand Claude's seeing that Creighton girl. Occasionally, I see them fly past in a blue convertible."

The woman now getting her hair styled said, "I can't see what a nice-looking man like Claude Calhoun sees in that Creighton girl. Why, she must be twenty years younger than him."

The other woman waiting said, "I'll tell you what he sees. He sees those long legs, that ample bust, and that firm tush. It's the same way I reeled in my John."

"Betty, your John never made it to market. You had him lassoed, separated, and branded before the rest of us entered the competition."

"That's right. But I was able to do it because he saw in me what he'd been looking for. Don't be surprised if this Creighton girl doesn't do the same to Claude. Did any of you ladies see him dance with that newspaper lady when Baxter Black and his big band came to town?"

"I did."

"Me too. I couldn't take my eyes off him. I think every woman in the ballroom watched as he left the newspaper lady's table and walked back to his."

"Okay, now. Did anyone see a young lady walk up and ask for his autograph?"

"No, I was taking my purse to Jerry for saying he didn't want to dance."

"I might have."

"Well, that girl was none other than Miss Meredith Creighton. You see ladies, when a woman sees something worth having, she bares her teeth and jumps into the fray. This Creighton woman started planning for Claude that very night. He'll be lucky if he lasts another six months."

"I've heard she's invited him to her house for the Thanksgiving meal. Probably wants to introduce him to her parents. Or maybe introduce her parents to him since she's already made up her mind."

When it was Adelle's turn, she opened the magazine to where her thumb held its place and said, "I want a hairstyle like Ava Gardner's."

Emmett arrived for lunch bringing a bottle of cheap wine. "Hello, Adelle. You . . . you look beautiful. Did you get the new hairdo for me?"

"No Emmett, I did it for someone else. But I waited too long to ask him, so it was either eat solo or call you. You barely edged out the alternative."

"Here." Emmett held out a bottle of wine. "And, there's no truth in the rumor of bewaring of Greeks bearing gifts."

"You're not Greek."

"Maybe not, but I do have a gift." Emmett followed Adelle into her kitchen. He had his nose held high and wasn't as much following Adelle as trying to track down those delicious aromas. "Whoa. What have we got here? Adelle, these cabinets are marvelous. I have to admit the Calhouns are the best carpenters in these parts."

"Emmett, here is your second rule. You and I are only friends. We are not engaged. Nor will we ever be. However, I do respect your opinion and I do find it pleasant to talk to you on occasion. Just remember your place, and everything will be okay."

"You got it. I was a little uncomfortable giving up my bachelorhood anyway. I'm too set in my ways to change for a woman."

"Careful."

CHAPTER 35—THE GILDED LILLY

"Boyd, how much did that brunette cost you last time?"

"Ten dollars, and I gave her a two-dollar tip."

Johnston Baker shifted down into second gear to go up a small hill. "I don't think I'll ever get used to this blooming Victory Speed. At thirty-five we could get passed by a fast bicycle." Coasting down the other side, Johnston shifted into third. "I think most of the women go for ten dollars, except for those two older ones."

Harold Greenleaf piped up from the back seat. "Yeah, them's mine. They go both for ten."

Mayor Bob sat next to Harold. "You tip them anything?"

"Naw, they're so glad to have someone ask, they'd probably work for free."

George Satterfield was sitting shotgun in the front seat. "Harold, why do you want two women? Do the three of you get into bed at the same time or do you finish with first one and then the other?"

"Now, George, a gentleman doesn't divulge the details. All I can say is, that first night in the interview room one of them whispered something in my ear, and—you know how hard of hearing I am—I just nodded. She motioned to the other and they led me upstairs giggling. From then, on I left everything up to them."

"Mayor, have you heard any more about Faisal's condition?"

Boyd said, "What condition?"

"Priapism. A severe swelling in his . . . with his . . . uh . . . the General."

"Is that what its called? I have Priapism every time I get with . . . uh . . . real often."

"No, Boyd. That's normal. This Priapism isn't normal. Faisal swells to a gigantic size. Two weeks ago it happened several mornings on his way to work. He hadn't done anything but eaten breakfast. Then last Tuesday morning, he woke up with it bigger than ever.

"Okay, I get it now. Faisal was the first one to come to the Gilded Lilly."

"Yep, Faisal went to the doctor when it happened the first time. The doctor looked up his condition in a book and said there was nothing he could do. And the women were on strike, so Faisal took it to the Gilded Lilly. I came with him that first night, and the next time Faisal had his problem, I called you guys. I'll bet none of you know, the girls don't charge him."

When Johnston and his four passengers arrived at the Gilded Lilly, the men got out of the car and stretched. It was only fifteen miles, but crowded together, five men in one car, was uncomfortable.

"There's Rube's car. He and Faisal are already here. Bob, we better hurry if you want that brunette. She's probably already standing in line for Faisal."

An hour later, a group of Skunk Hollow men surrounded the house. Fifteen in total, they planned on whipping the asses of the seven men from Dancing Deer. Someone from the house had called, saying the men from Dancing Deer were molesting Skunk Hollow women. The caller was the same person who bet Harold Greenleaf the New York Hotshots would beat the Dancing Deer Peckerwoods in a game of baseball. The Peckerwoods won, the Skunk Hollow woman lost, and now, she would have her revenge.

Waiting on the brunette, Boyd was the only man not with a woman. He was sitting on the front porch by himself when five cars drove up at the same time. Men carrying clubs streamed out with blood in their eyes. They started congregating in one seething mass. Boyd ran into the house and ascended the stairs.

He opened first one door and then another yelling, "Every man in Skunk Hollow is coming to kill us. Find something to fight with and get to the top of the stairs." After three doors, the other doors opened on their own with men holding onto the doorknobs and trying desperately to get an article or two of clothing on.

Boyd grabbed a shirt, "Throw your wallets in here."

"Why?"

"Do it and then find something to fight with. Forget the clothes, you can fight naked. Like the Greeks."

152

Boyd tied the shirttail and sleeves together over the wallets and keys. He ran to the bathroom. When he came out he wasn't carrying the shirt. "Look, there's more of them than of us, so we'll do it like the Greeks at Thermopylae. They'll have to come up the stairs to get us, so grab a chair to cover your head and we'll form a Hoplite Phalanx by interlocking the chairs. Each of you stick a leg of your chair through the one to your left. Okay men, let's bunch up at the first landing. Harold, you, Mayor Bob, and Rube stay at the top. If one makes it by our defensive line, the three of you have to drag him up and toss his butt over the railing. If anyone on the landing gets hurt, you guys drag him up to the top and one of you have to take his place. Okay, let's go."

The front door burst open, and fifteen angry men stormed in. They saw the men from Dancing Deer on the stairs and headed their way. The first of the Skunk Hollow men up the stairs met more than he had bargained for. The men from Dancing Deer fought from a superior position, and only two of the Skunk Hollow men could assail their defenses at a time.

George Satterfield was the first to get in a good lick. He sent a man tumbling back into the ones waiting their turn. Boyd reached through his chair and grabbed a man's club. Boyd pulled and the man came with it, only to be smashed in the side of his face by a broken chair leg. Johnston was a big man with big hands. The women liked him because he was so big. Of course, he was small potatoes compared to Faisal. But when he made a fist, it was a big fist. Several men from Skunk Hollow felt the knuckles of that big fist against their faces. The men from Skunk Hollow fell back. Three of their number were now incapacitated. They huddled, then yelled at the men from Dancing Deer to come outside so The Gilded Lilly wouldn't suffer any damage.

"We didn't start the fight. Go on home if you don't want the joint busted up."

"Okay, men, let's get 'em." They charged again, but after several minutes, it was with the same outcome and the men from Skunk Hollow fell back a second time. Then they walked outside on the porch to plan a new strategy. A woman yelled something from a second-story window. With their third effort the belligerents from Skunk Hollow came back with renewed energy. During the ensuing melee, Harold Greenleaf was knocked from the top landing. Several men from Skunk

Hollow had climbed onto the roof and came in a bedroom window. They attacked Harold and the Dancing Deer men held in reserve from behind. Soon the men from Dancing Deer were all on the first landing with some of the men from Skunk Hollow attacking from below and others attacking from above.

Johnston was knocked down with a club. Rube tossed a man over the railing. George knocked out a man's false teeth and Faisal bit holes in the lobe of a man's ear. Boyd was knocked into the back wall and received a kick to the face on his way to the floor. Mayor Bob lowered his head and plowed into the lead man on the stairs. He ended up knocking every man below the landing to the floor. Because of this, he became known as Mayor Bob the Bull. Johnston got to his feet and picked up Boyd. The men from Dancing Deer then pressed their advantage on the Skunk Hollow men sprawled around on the floor below.

In a few minutes, Boyd and six almost-naked men, stood in a tight circle holding chairs and clubs. The front door opened and in walked the Pope County sheriff and two deputies with their guns pulled.

"Everybody, get your hands up. Throw down those clubs. Now, against the wall. Everybody, that means you too, Dennis. We're going to wait until the paddy wagons get here. You gentlemen will be spending the rest of Thanksgiving as guests of the Pope County judicial system."

"Sir, may we get our clothes?"

"No, I think you look fine." The sheriff shook his head and started looking at the damage to The Gilded Lilly, He said, "Any of you gentlemen have identification?"

"No."

"None."

"Me either."

"Who owns those cars?"

"They were here when we arrived."

"Yeah, they're not ours."

"How'd you get here?"

"Walked."

"I don't believe that."

"Not me. I rode a horse then shooed him home after I got off."

"Okay, What's your name?"

"John Smith."

"What's yours."

Mayor Bob the Bull stood straight, in faded red long johns. He shrugged his shoulders and said, "Bill McAdams. My uncle is Judge McAdams."

"Okay, McAdams, you go with Deputy Butz and give your statement."

"Dennis, you want to give your side of the story to Deputy Smith?"

"Looks like the wagons are here. Everybody outside." The sheriff looked at the top of the stairs. "Betts, I'll need for you to come down tomorrow and file a complaint." She nodded.

In the hullabaloo of everyone going out the front door and loading into the paddy wagons Boyd stepped behind a large potted plant and watched as his friends were loaded. He waited thirty minutes while the girls put their house in order. He then stepped inside and asked what had happened.

"Not tonight, sonny. We're closed for the rest of the weekend. Come back Monday."

"Can I have the clothes of my friends from Dancing Deer?"

"Yeah, sure. They're in a pile in the kitchen."

"Listen, if you won't press charges, we'll repair your place. It was the other men's fault anyway."

"Yeah, but they could have left and had the brawl in the front yard like the men from Skunk Hollow asked. How come you're not loaded up with the rest?"

"I wasn't in the fight. I came afterwards."

"Oh, yeah, what about that skinned nose and that swollen ear?"

"Hang on, I got to check it out." Boyd shot up the stairs to the bathroom where he retrieved the hidden shirt with the wallets. Coming downstairs, he said, "I don't know how that happened."

"Ma'am, we're good carpenters. If you won't press charges, we'll fix it up better than new."

"Let me think about it."

155

.

CHAPTER 36—POPE COUNTY JAIL

Twenty-one men were led from the paddy wagons to central booking at the Pope County Jail. They were asked to remove their jewelry, billfolds, and other items from their pockets. Everything produced was placed in numbered envelopes. The corresponding number on a slip of paper was given to each man and told he'd need the ticket to retrieve his stuff when released.

Each man had an opportunity to give his name and place of residence. Each was then photographed, fingerprinted, allowed one telephone call, and stuffed into a large holding cell. A toilet was bolted to the floor in the center of the cell with a roll of toilet paper sitting nearby on the floor.

Outside the cell area, two deputies discussed their predicament. "Out of the twenty-one belligerents, we can only identify sixteen. The other five say their names are John Smith and they live on the street."

"Who do you reckon they really are?"

"Don't know. Maybe Betts will tell us when she gets here to sign the complaint."

"What about the identification on the cars?"

"Five cars, all registered to citizens of Skunk Hollow."

Inside the cell area, the prisoners divided into two hostile groups sitting on the concrete floor with their backs turned to each other. Leaning against the concrete block wall or the iron bars, they huddled with no one having the inclination to use the porcelain fixture.

In the smaller of the two groups, Faisal said, "I'd say we're in a world of hurt. Did anyone make a telephone call?"

"I didn't. By now the women are in City Park for the lighting of the town Christmas tree."

"What kind of excuse will they give for us not being there?"

Mayor Bob the Bull moaned. "The mayor has always made a speech at the lighting of the tree. We were only supposed to be gone long enough for a quickie and then be back in plenty of time for the ceremony. I didn't even give Clarice an excuse for leaving. I caught her busy with the clean-up of the gymnasium and slipped out."

George Satterfield said, "That's pretty much the way I handled it as well."

Rube added, "You guys are worthless. I didn't feel obligated to say anything to anybody. Suzanne left before I did, saying she didn't mind preparing the food or feeding the people attending, but drew the line at cleaning up."

Johnston said, "I tried to call Betty, but there was no answer."

There were several hundred people at City Park, but only four members of the city council and no master of ceremony. Paul Nelson searched for the other members, but could only find Ed Stanky, Jerry Millhouse, and Stone.

Clarice gathered the women for a conference. She said, "So, where the hell are they?"

Imogene Greenleaf said, "Harold told me he was going over to your house for a few minutes. He said he'd be back around six, in plenty of time for us to attend the ceremony at seven."

"Well, he wasn't coming to see me. Maybe he met Robert somewhere else. Betty, where's your John?

"Lost."

"Ophelia?"

"Clarice, Faisal said he was headed to your house."

"Gladys, why isn't Edwin missing like the rest of the men?"

"Because Eddy doesn't get into trouble. He was with me all afternoon. After cleaning up the gym we went home. He said his back was aching from carrying those big pots so I gave him a massage."

"You what?"

"Yeah, I sent off for some ointment that gets warm when applied and I rubbed it on his back. I've bought this book on giving massages and now I do it all the time, but usually on his legs and feet."

"That's ridiculous. I'd never give Rube a massage. He doesn't deserve it."

"Eddy does."

"Gladys, go ask Edwin where our men are."

"I know where they are. He's already told me, but I didn't want to say anything."

"You didn't want to tell us?"

"No. It's . . . uh, embarrassing."

"Too late for that. Go ahead and tell us. We need to know. Robert is supposed to light the tree . . ." Clarice Springer looked down at her watch. "in fifteen minutes."

"They said they were going to the Gilded Lilly and asked Eddy if he'd like to go."

"The Gilded Lilly? Our husbands are at a whorehouse? I don't believe it."

"I do. That explains a lot."

"I'm going to kill my John."

"Ladies, we have to remain calm and get out of this situation with a little dignity. And we still have the lighting ceremony. We'll have to deal with the men later."

"Who's going to light the tree? And who's going to make the speech?"

"I think we should turn it over to the four members who are here. Paul could probably do it. Gladys, what about Edwin?"

"Poor Eddy stammers when he has to talk in front of a crowd. I think we ought to ask Paul."

Clarice held up her hands. "I don't. I'm going to give the damned speech. And Suzanne can flip the switch for the tree. Ladies, it's time for the women to take charge."

CHAPTER 37—DEMAS TO THE RESCUE

The men combed the woods for Cameron—and for W.W. Wainwright, of course. James Pike said he needed to stay with the barge so Jim, Bear, and the two ladies went north and east of the cabin while Horace Honeycut and John went due north.

As soon as they were out the door, Tarleton asked Demas if he needed any help feeding the animals. Every family in the country had chickens for eggs, a cow or goats for milk, and a hog for disposing of the table scraps and for slaughter.

"Why'd you do it? I thought we were friends."

"We are, Demas. I saw his poster in Brewster and thought he might be dangerous. They offered a reward of a thousand dollars. I thought he'd killed someone."

"Well, he didn't. You heard what that woman said. She's the one offering the reward. They were supposed to have gotten married. All Tom did was fall off a train."

"I know that now, but I didn't when I thought he was hid out from the law in your house. I thought I was saving your life."

"Thanks a lot. Now I'll never learn to read."

"If you really want it that bad I'll use some of the reward money to bring in a teacher from Brewster. All three of us can learn."

"Where'd you get the glasses, Tarleton?"

"Mom asked me to thread her needle. I told her it had two eyes and she made Dad take me to have mine checked. That's when I saw the poster." Tarleton was carrying the slop bucket, and when they reached the shed that housed the animals, he poured its contents into a hollowed-out log. "When we finish, let's find Cameron and Tom—just you and me. Those others don't know nothing about these woods like we do." Tarleton bent down and picked up Radix. "We got Cameron's coat. Let's see if Radix can scent him out." He scratched behind Radix's ears.

Katy and Faye were having a hard time keeping up with Bear and Jim, so while they were still close to the cabin, they decided to go back and help Charley fix the Thanksgiving meal.

After the animals were fed, Tarleton and Demas left as Faye and Katy were arriving. Tarleton carried Cameron's coat and Demas carried one end of a rope with the other end tied around Radix's neck.

"Demas, we were traveling the west trail when I stepped on a pile of tacks. You had them camouflaged real good. I hobbled back to your house while they continued. At almost dark, John the camera guy arrived saying he was through, that he'd been hauled high in a tree and he didn't care if they caught the man or not. He said Cameron went on while Mr. Honeycut tried to figure a way to get him down. So that means Cameron probably made it to your next trap."

There was a loud blast. "Get down, someone's shooting."

"Naw. That's just one of my gimmicks. In several places, I wedged shotgun shells in forks of trees. When I had one stuck pretty tight, I placed a wad of mud to cover the striking point and shoved in a tack. Then I rigged up a large rock on a pivoting stick held in place with thread. When someone came along and broke the thread, the pivoting stick slammed down with the rock hitting the tack head and firing the shell. I had the shell pointing up in the trees. It wasn't meant to hurt anyone, just scare."

"Demas, you ought to write a book."

"I got to learn to read one first."

Radix pulled on the rope with his nose to the ground. Pretty soon he dug in a pile of leaves. A small mouse scurried away and hid under the exposed root of a large tree. Demas tugged on the rope.

"Yep, here's where that camera man went up the tree. Tarleton, let him sniff the coat again."

Radix pulled the two boys along with his head held high in the air. Every now and then, he stopped to sniff a bush crowding the path. More than once, he covered a previous scent with his.

"Tarleton, watch your step. I got a trap here somewhere."

Tarleton stopped and Demas picked up Radix. "Let's walk off the path for a few feet. There's one here somewhere. I just can't remember exactly where or what kind."

Fifty feet farther, Demas said they could get back on the path. Another shotgun blast broke the November stillness.

Tarleton and Demas started ascending a rocky ridge with tall trees and thick underbrush on their left. On their right was a deep ravine with steep and rocky sides. "I remember putting something here as well. It was a tree limb. Look, it's been triggered." From their right, a half mile or so away, a man screamed.

Radix stopped and looked down into the rugged and deep ditch. Demas tugged on the rope, "Come on, boy." Radix wouldn't budge.

"Demas, that branch probably knocked Cameron down into this gulley. Let's go down."

"Okay, but take it slow and go from one of those scraggly bushes to another. There's hardly any soil, so you'll slide in the broken bits of rock."

"Don't you think he would've left foot prints?"

"Not if he was falling."

Both boys and the little dog descended the rocky slope. When they got to the bottom, a creek flowed in a narrow level area. There were a few trees and other bits of vegetation. On the other side of the creek, another slope headed back up.

"You ever been down here?"

"Yeah, there's a small cave over there." Demas pointed behind them.

"Let's go check it out. I don't see any other areas where someone could hide."

Charley had several pots cooking on her wood stove. James brought in tins of meat and sacks of fresh vegetables. Faye and Katy sat in chairs and watched the entire operation.

The front door blew open and John the camera man stepped inside carrying Horace Honeycut. "Young lady, is there somewhere I can lay him?"

"Sure, on Tom's pallet, by the fire."

"What happened?" asked Faye.

"I'm not sure. We were going down a narrow path when the ground started moving. I think it was a net or maybe cord tied together in some sort of grid. Anyway, I jumped off but Horace got his foot entangled. He slid down the path for twenty or thirty feet, then left, airborne. He landed in a tree. There was a rope tied to whatever he got caught in and at its terminus was stuck through a hole in a boulder going down the path at breakneck speed. I could see it in the distance. I'm glad he got caught in the tree or he might still be sliding feet first down the path behind that boulder." John laid his boss on the pallet. "Do you have anything to drink?"

"Yeah." Charley looked at the newspaper man, now sitting up on the pallet. "Mister, what would you like?"

"Not for him, for me. From now on, he can fend for himself."

Katy walked to the newspaper editor. She reached down and unlaced the shoe on his hurt foot. She removed the shoe and sock and then rolled up his pants leg. She ran her fingers softly over the crest of his foot. She moved the foot up and down and then sideways. Horace grimaced. She lowered his foot. "You got a sprained ankle, Mr. Honeycut." Katy walked back to her sister and said, "I should've learned to cook."

Faye said, "Me too, but you know mom. She thought cooking was work and pampered us to the point we weren't good for anything. After W.W. and I get married I'm going to take cooking lessons. Before you know it, I'll be known as a regular homemaker."

"Can a leopard really change its spots?"

"It depends on the motivation. I've already had a decent career. I've now got a book about to be published. I think it's time to have a family before I'm too old."

"What about W.W? Is he not already too old?"

"He's physically fit and has a good sense of humor. If he is too old, he'll still enjoy the effort. I suppose we could adopt. But only as a last resort. What about you?"

"Bear and I enjoy each other's company but there's too much difference in our ages. I'm eighteen years older than he. While he might think I'm pretty now, in twenty years he'll reach middle age and I'll be an old woman. I think what we have is nice and I'm enjoying every minute of it, but I have to be realistic. Right now, he doesn't see it that way and that's fine with me, but I can't let it get out of hand. No long-term commitments. I wish it were different."

"W.W. is fifteen years older than me. So you might say you and I have the same problem, except reversed. Where I can live with an older man I love, you think the younger man won't love you when you get old. Maybe the two of you should talk about it."

"That big guy is your boyfriend?" Horace rolled down his pants leg.

"Yes. Almost. Well, not quite. So far we've found ourselves accidentally thrown together in oddball circumstances."

In the distance, there was another shotgun blast.

"You ought to find someone fun to be around. Someone with a little more experience."

"The pickings are mighty poor for that age group in my town," said Katy.

"Demas, look at Radix." Radix had stepped into the cave, tugged on the rope, and growled.

"I think that big guy is in there."

"Don't go in there, Tarleton. There might be a painter or a wolverine."

"Let's go in a few feet and see if we can make anything out."

"I'd feel better if we had one of the men with us."

"Come on, Demas."

"Okay, but I'm going to tie Radix outside with a knot he can untie with a little effort."

The two boys lowered their heads and walked in the four-foot opening.

"Shhh. Be real quiet. I'm under a bear."

Tarleton and Demas were speechless. After a moment, Demas whispered, "How can we help you?"

"I don't know. He's almost awake, and he's holding me down with his arm."

"Mister, we'll be right back. I've got an idea."

Back outside, Tarleton said, "Why did you tie Radix like that?"

"If there was a mountain lion or wolverine in there, and we got hurt somehow, I didn't want Radix to be unable to get free."

"Okay, what're we going to do about Cameron?"

"You stay right here. I've got to get a crutch." Demas used his pocketknife to cut a forked branch. He then picked up a large piece of dead wood and cut a hole in its middle. He kept working on the hole until it allowed the first branch to pass all the way through. Back at the cave he said, "Tarleton, you got to hold Radix while I go in. If he follows me in he could rouse the bear."

"I won't let him get away."

Demas untied Radix and handed his little dog to Tarleton. With one hand holding the rope, Demas stuffed the big man's coat under his arm and used his other hand to pick up the stick and large piece of dead wood. Holding his items and shaking, Demas entered the cave. Crouching beside the man, he whispered. "Mister, turn on your side."

Cameron squirmed, finally getting on his side. Demas measured from the bear's arm to the floor and used his knife to cut off part of the forked stick. He slid the stick into the piece of dead wood and wrapped the coat around the fork. Sliding the coat and the fork in the dead piece of wood under the bear's arm Demas then whispered, "Give me a second to get out, then turn over on your back. When you're ready, let out all your air and give me a tug on the rope. With your stomach flattened as low as possible Tarleton and I should be able to pull you free. When you do get free, don't make any quick movements. Be real slow getting out. Are you ready?"

"Yeah. Son if this works, I'll owe you my life."

"If it doesn't is there anything you want me to say at your funeral?"

"Yeah, I didn't mean to cause anybody no harm . . . and . . . son, don't you think this is going to work?"

A few minutes later two little boys, one little dog, and one very mean man—who was not feeling mean at the moment—scrambled up a rocky slope.

After wandering in the woods for an hour and being lost in the woods for two hours, Bear and Jim Pike found themselves back at the cabin.

"Man, we must've been walking in circles. If your Mr. Wainwright is out here, he's probably lost too."

"Possibly. Let's go inside and get something to drink. We'll rest a spell, then head out again."

When they opened the door, the two hunters were bombarded with the smells of a home-cooked meal. In the corner sat Horace Honeycut nursing a swollen ankle. Around the table sat John the camera man, James, Faye, Katy, and someone Bear had not seen before. He held out his hand. "I'm Bear Radisson."

The stranger got to his feet and shook Bear's hand. "Welcome to my home. I'm Chester."

The young girl was the only one doing any work. Bear walked over to a bucket and drank from a gourd ladle. "Where's those two boys?"

The door opened and in staggered the two boys, one under each arm of a rather large and dirty man.

Honeycut said, "Hey, Cameron. It's good to see you. Where've you been?"

James stood up and gave Cameron his chair.

"Thanks, Mr. Pike. Boy, do I have a story to tell. This young man . . ." he looked around the room. "Now where'd he go? Anyway . . . . as I was saying . . ."

Demas walked to the water's edge and got into his father's boat. He paddled to the other side and walked down a hidden trail. Soon he and Tom were squatting around a small fire.

"Tom, your name is Wayne Winchell Wainwright. You go by W.W. You were a cop in New York City, Chicago, and some little town in Northern Arkansas. You were in a train wreck and fell from a trestle into the river. You floated here. That's all I know, except that there's a woman saying you and she were going to get married."

"You sure, Demas? It sounds a little far-fetched to me."

"How about I bring the woman and you decide for yourself. I'll come in from downstream. No one will know you're only a hundred yards away." Demas paused for a moment, then said, "In about fifteen minutes you crawl down by the water's edge. Maybe you'll hear her talk."

"Okay, but if you bring her over, you need to stay handy in case I decide to send her back."

CHAPTER 38—CLARICE FOR MAYOR

"Ladies and gentlemen, it's time to light the Dancing Deer Christmas tree. Normally, the mayor gives a speech to formally open the holiday season. This year my husband, Mayor Bob, has been called away on an emergency errand. He's asked me if I would stand in and speak on his behalf.

"This past year, Dancing Deer has gone through a metamorphosis. Your city government led the way—actually pulling along those hesitant to move with us. We've been at the forefront, even instrumental, in beautifying our picturesque little city. We have the new City Park with piped-in music. We have a thermal spring, built to supply recreation the year 'round, along with lighted, winding walkways, and other water features. Besides the park, the city now sports a wide walking boulevard with newly planted trees and public restrooms. And, as the crowning point, the families of the same people you elected to run your city have painted eighty percent of the storefronts along Main Street. Dancing Deer truly is the prettiest little town in the Ozarks." Clarice had to wait for the applause to die down.

"As wife of the mayor, I can tell you that during the remaining year in office your city government is planning additional improvements." Clarice paused while the audience clapped again. Soon she continued with, "At all times, but especially at this time of year, we need to show steadfast faith in our God, and in our country. We need to forgive those who have offended us, to have charity in our hearts—and in our pocketbooks—for those less fortunate, to have hope in the future for our children, and to have boundless love for all mankind.

"Suzanne, would you flip the switch for Dancing Deer's Christmas tree." Clarice paused while the lights were turned off, the volume on the address system turned up, and the tree lights energized. When the entire area began twinkling by reflecting the light from thousands of colorful lights adorning the tree, Clarice leaned close to the microphone and said, "I hereby declare this holiday season open. Please patronize your local businesses."

Clarice stepped back amid thunderous applause. Ophelia said, "Clarice, did I hear you correctly? You gave the credit for the city improvements to our husbands. Instead, those improvements were accomplished in spite of their best efforts?"

"Why not? Who's going to argue?"

"I think you ought to run for mayor. We'd help. Maybe, we could continue with the city improvements our husbands have tried to stymie."

"I agree."

"Me too."

The next morning was the Friday after Thanksgiving and Boyd went into the Pope County Jail in Russellville, twenty miles from Skunk Hollow. "I have some friends who spent the night in your jail by mistake. Is there any chance they'll be released today?"

The deputy in charge of booking looked up from a tall stack of urgent messages. "They haven't been charged with anything. They were outside any city limits and it appears no one had been drinking. So, unless Betts McGowan presses charges for damages to her house, they'll be released by five this afternoon. I've been told that Betts has the entire day to appear.

"May I speak with them?"

"Depends. You have a name?"

Boyd thought for a moment. "Yeah, John Smith."

"We got five of them. Any one in particular?"

"No, they're all brothers."

"Someone names five sons with the same first name?"

"Yeah, crazy, isn't it? I think they got different middle names."

Soon Boyd was led down the hall to the holding cell. His friends were in a corner. Boyd walked over to talk with them through the bars. "You characters are in a fix. Your wives are going to kill you when you return and the citizens of Dancing Deer are thinking about recalling you from office. The Dancing Deer Police and the Marsden County Sheriff's Office are also looking for you. And Betts McGowan claims you started the fight and wants thirty-thousand dollars to repair the damage."

"Thirty-thousand dollars? We didn't tear nothing up but those stairs and a few chairs."

"Those stairs were built around a central pole holding up the roof. It fell in last night after you left."

"The entire roof collapsed?"

"Yep. Brought down four chimneys and three of the four exterior walls. Did I say that the Pope County judge is her best customer? He's madder'n hell."

Harold Greenleaf started pushing Mayor Bob the Bull. "You jackass. I wouldn't have come without your coercion."

"Me neither. Damnit, Bob. We ought to thrash your hide."

Boyd added, "Now, hold on, boys. What if I was to say that I talked her out of pressing charges in return for a little carpentry work?"

"I'd name my first-born in your honor."

"Your first born was a girl, and you named her Peggy Sue."

"Yes, but I'd tell everyone it was done in your honor."

"Okay, look, I'm not entirely certain she's going to bypass showing up and pressing charges, but I did promise we'd make a few repairs to her house."

"That's all right. We can do the carpentry work. Does it mean completely rebuilding the place?"

"Naw, I was just fooling with you."

"Boyd!"

"You guys owe me. I hid both cars before the sheriff came back to get their license plate numbers. They're outside parked across the street. And I got your pants and wallets in their trunks. If she doesn't show up, they're going to release you this afternoon. You'll have to streak outside, but I'll have the doors unlocked. I don't think you should tell them about the wallets or cars. So far they don't know who the hell you are, and I think we ought to keep it that way. They think you're all brothers, all John Smiths with different middle names."

"Yeah, I want my real name kept out of it."

"Me too. I can be a John Smith for a while."

"I just want to go home."

"All right, you guys stay warm. I'll be right outside when they release you."

"Boyd, could I have your shirt? I ain't got nothing."

The men watched Boyd, now naked to the waist, as he left then started talking about the excuses they should give the women. Harold was the loudest, "I think we should say we had car trouble."

"Doing what?"

"Buying a farm for investment."

"Okay, but if they don't buy it, we could say we were giving Boyd his first lesson in manhood. We were just delivering him to a bevy of lusty wenches. We weren't partaking ourselves, of course."

Makepeace Kilburn was mending a fence when his wife came home with two sacks of groceries. "You'll never guess who they got locked up in the county jail."

"Who?"

"Fifteen of our finest citizens, five John Smiths, and one Bill McAdams."

"What for?"

"Busting up the Gilded Lilly."

"You got the names of our citizens?"

"A few."

"And these five John Smiths? You know anything about them?"

"Supposedly, they're all brothers. Their parents kept up with them by giving each a different middle name."

"I've heard of everything now. Where they from?"

"None had any identification. Said they were just passing through."

"Okay, what about the one named McAdams?"

"He's supposed to be kin to the judge in Marsden County, but the judge denies it."

"Maybe I should go into town and take some pictures. There could be a story here."

At four-thirty, Betts McGowan had not shown up, and the officer in charge of booking started releasing his prisoners. First the fifteen men from Skunk Hollow sauntered out. Then the front door to the jail opened just a little and a middle-aged man wearing long-handle bottoms ran out the door, across a busy street, and jumped into the back seat of a black Ford.

"George, they right behind you?"

"Yeah, just takes a minute. I almost signed my real name. We didn't have much for them to give back. I think they got three watches and that's it."

The front door opened and Johnston Baker came running out in jockey shorts and a t-shirt. Makepeace had his camera sitting on a tripod and snapped two pictures before Johnston made it all the way to the car. People started collecting on the sidewalk to see who would come charging out next. It was Rube. He wore a long-tailed shirt with nothing underneath. The camera started snapping pictures as fast as Makepeace could focus. Faisal Obadiah and Harold Greenleaf followed on his heels in similar dress. Then Mayor Bob opened the door and walked out. He smiled for the camera, waved at the crowd, and strutted to the Ford. He wore a faded red union suit with the flap buttoned shut.

"Boyd, let's go. That's everyone. How come our clothes aren't in the car?"

"I didn't think there'd be enough room to get dressed. They're in the trunk. I'll find a place outside of town and stop."

"Johnston, you're taking up too much of the seat."

"Harold! Man, you smell bad."

"Okay, that's enough. We got to get along for another hour."

CHAPTER 39—CLAUDE SHOWS AN INTEREST

Emmett didn't stay long after the meal. Adelle decided to start decorating her house for Christmas and Emmett made an excuse saying he needed to check on his parents. Adelle pulled out a box of Christmas tree ornaments and sat in her most comfortable chair. Two hours later, Adelle was sleeping soundly when someone knocked on the door.

Adelle opened her eyes, realized it was late afternoon, and walked wearily to the door. "Hello, Claude. Come in. I didn't expect to see you today."

"I came by to make sure you're happy with the cabinets."

They walked into the kitchen. Adelle ran her index finger along the countertop. "I couldn't be happier. You're a good carpenter." Adelle picked up a clean bowl and put it behind a golden oak door with a glass insert. "I think I'm going to have to wash everything before putting it up. Do you think I should put down shelf paper?" Adelle picked up another bowl and began washing it in the sink.

"No. The wood's tight-grained. With the shellac it won't soak up any water. Can I help you?" Claude picked up the washed bowl and began drying it with a clean dishtowel.

"Claude, I don't know what I've done with my manners. Let's go into the living room. I was about to start decorating the Christmas tree."

"Don't you want to do the dishes first?"

"No, I can do them after you leave. Right now, I'd like for you to sit in my grandfather's big chair and talk to me while I decorate the tree. But first, let me make us a drink. With the cold and the wind, I think I'd like a hot buttered rum. Is that all right with you?"

"Sounds great."

Adelle took Claude's hand and led him into the living room.

"Is there anything I can do?" asked Claude.

175

"You can take the ornaments out of the newspaper wrapping and set each on the coffee table. While you're doing that, I'll fix the drinks."

Claude held up one of the ornaments to the light of a lamp. "These are exquisite. I haven't seen anything like them in the shops."

"I know. I picked them up, one at a time, from all over the world. There's also a box on the floor with a hand-carved nativity scene from the Black Forest in Germany. I shudder to think what's happened to that quaint little village. Probably been bombed from the face of the planet."

"Everybody loses in war."

"Claude, you're so deep and mysterious. It's no wonder the women hang all over you."

"I'm just a country boy. I build things. I haven't been anywhere or accomplished anything. All I've ever done is read books and dream."

"That's precisely what every woman wants: a good-looking dreamer with an ability to make and appreciate beautiful things."

"Would he be a person you might find interesting?"

"Claude, you're also someone who has a marketable skill. I understand your construction company is going great guns."

"Yes, the boys are coming home and wanting to build houses for their new families."

"And you have the supply of lumber tied up so you and Rupert are the only ones capable of building those houses."

"Adelle, you make it sound sinister."

"No, I'm astonished at your business acumen. I don't think you're just a country boy. You could be a Carnegie or a Mellon or even a Rothschild disguised as a country boy. Here, try this." Adelle handed Claude a mug with steam coming off the top. "Better let it cool for a minute."

"I noticed there were dishes for two. Are you still seeing Emmett?"

"No, I had planned on calling you but heard at the beauty salon women are now taking numbers and waiting their turn. So I got in line. Claude, I'm now the third one on your list. But since you were tied up for the moment, I called Emmett and told him, as long as both of us were by ourselves, we should eat together. At least, there would be someone to talk to."

"Adelle, that's not fair. So far I've asked you out and been turned down. I've asked to carry your colors and had to play second fiddle to someone who only wanted your money. I don't need your money. I just want to get to know you better. You want to step to the head of the line?"

"Yes, I do." She walked over to where he was standing, reached up and cradled his face with her hands, and kissed him on the lips. "There, I've wanted to do that since the time you chased down my hat."

"Don't stop now."

CHAPTER 40—THE MEN ARRIVE

After stopping and putting on their clothes, the men from Dancing Deer started feeling more at ease now that each wasn't sitting so close to another naked man. Johnston took over the controls to his Ford. "Boyd, I don't suppose you know how the ceremony went last night?"

"Just what they were saying at the diner. Clarice gave the speech and Suzanne lit the tree. There's now a petition going around endorsing Bob's wife to run for mayor in next year's elections."

"What about me? I was planning on running again," lamented Bob.

"Most people are now of the opinion your wife will do a better job. Some of the other women want their own seats on the city council as well. It's a new world dawning, Mayor Bob."

"Hey, who's that?"

"I don't know. Let's stop and offer her a lift."

Johnston slowed his car and rolled down his window at the same time. "Hey gorgeous. Uh . . . hello, Gladys. What are you doing?"

"I'm jogging. I'm glad to see you boys are okay. Last night when you didn't show at the ceremony, we got to worrying. Are you just now getting back?"

"Yeah. What are you jogging for?"

"It's good exercise. It firms up the legs and takes inches off the waist."

"Can we offer you a ride into town?"

"Now, where would I sit? No, don't answer that. I got two more miles to go. See you guys later."

"We can make room for you in the back."

Gladys shook her head, picked up speed, and left them with their mouths open.

Johnston let George Satterfield off first. They waited. In a few minutes, George appeared at the door, shrugged his shoulders, and went back inside his house.

"Maybe it's not as bad as we feared." Mayor Bob settled back in his seat. His house was the second stop. He jumped out of the car and ran into the house. In a minute he was back at the car. "She left a note saying she and some of the other ladies were in town shopping. For me not to go anywhere and to have supper fixed when she returned."

Harold said, "This does not bode well."

"It doesn't bother me any. My girlfriend isn't on my bank account and I don't have open credit at any of the retail stores. She can shop all she wants."

"Boyd, when'd you get so nasty?"

The next house belonged to Boyd. Someone had built a fire in his front yard. There was a big black circle fringed with bits and pieces of charred clothing: A shirtsleeve here, a pants leg there, one cowboy boot standing in the middle, still smoldering.

"Damn, she's burned my clothes, and . . . and we're not even married."

Johnston took Harold home last. Harold looked around for a moment before he opened his car door. "I don't see anything wrong." Then he saw her. At the edge of his porch. His mother-in-law. "Oh, hell, no. I had her in a nursing home. Well, my life is spiraling down. See you, Johnston. I hope you do better."

When Johnston arrived at his house, he parked the Ford and headed in through the back door. "Now what's wrong with this key?" After fiddling for a few minutes he decided to try the front door. "Good Lord, she's had the locks re-keyed."

CHAPTER 41—DEMAS LEADS FAYE

When Demas walked through the door, Cameron stood up. "Son, I been telling everyone how smart you are. Come over here, you can have my seat."

"Thank you sir, but I need to talk with the lady."

"What is it, Demas?"

"Let's step outside, ma'am."

When Demas and Faye went through the front door several conversations started inside at the same time. "I think he knows where Wainwright is."

"The kid's the smartest one here."

"If he doesn't want Wainwright found, he won't be. In fact, he's laid so many traps I'm afraid to go looking anymore."

"Me, too. I've had two close calls and been hauled up a tree once."

Horace Honeycut said, "He's just a little boy."

Tarleton retorted. "Can you determine when the full moon will come, how to tie a bowline or a sheepshank, tell north by the stars? Demas can. He might not be book smart but he knows things. He pays attention. He's my best friend, and I'm going to use my reward money to hire a teacher so Demas can learn to read and write."

Outside, Demas led Faye to the dock where there were three make-shift chairs. "Let's talk about Tom."

W.W. sat behind a bush on the other side of the river. The water made the conversation carry. Tom decided he'd have to be quiet because, if he could hear them, they could hear him just as easy.

Faye said, "What do you want to know?"

"I want to feel comfortable that you mean him no harm."

"I love him. I wouldn't hurt him for anything. Here, I've got a letter from him in my pocket. Do you want to see it?"

"No, I'll take your word for it. Are you younger than him?"

"Yes, by fifteen years. I'm forty. Old, by an unmarried woman's standards. W.W. is the man I've been running from my entire life. He caught me in New York City. We're soul mates, meant for each other. You know, he's famous in the big city. He was going to be the New York City Chief of Police. I don't know what he'll want to do now, but whatever it is, I'll be with him propping him up."

"Okay, I'll take you to him. He still doesn't remember anything before Daddy untangled him from our fishing line. And he doesn't look much like the guy in the picture. He might not even be your man, though I hope he is."

Demas stood up. "We got to get in the boat and travel downstream a ways." He held the boat still while Faye negotiated the step from the dock to the small john-boat.

"I'm so excited, I feel like a little girl being given a pony. Is it far?"

"No, not far." Demas didn't have to do much paddling. He used his paddle to keep the boat traveling in a straight line and in the middle where the current was strongest.

"How was he teaching you to read?"

"He taught Charley and me how to sound out words. He said it was a matter of recognition. After you figured out how a particular word sounded, the next time you saw the word you'd recognize it and say it the proper way without having to go through the process again. He made us pause when we came to a comma and to stop altogether at periods, then start up again. We got three Nancy Drew books and one Hardy Boys adventure. Charley is better than me. She uses a candle and sounds out words long into the night. I tried it once and caught my covers on fire."

Demas pulled the boat into a quiet cove and hauled it halfway onto the bank. "Watch your step. We don't come over here much. The only paths are made by animals and there're blackberry bushes with stickers everywhere. In the fall, we sit on the dock and see bears going from one bush to another. They're not afraid of humans, so Charley has to be careful with the kitchen scraps. Last year I decided to feed the scraps with meat to the fish. She now separates the meat scraps and gives our hog everything else. We then haul the portion with meat to the end of the dock and put them in a wire basket. Every time she hauls it up, it's empty except for the bones and Radix gets those."

"Demas, I'm afraid of bears."

"You don't have to be this time of year. They're sleeping till spring. Just ask Cameron." A few feet further along the trail, Demas stopped. "Here's where I leave you. He's in the next clearing. Good luck, ma'am."

Faye reached out and grabbed Demas. She pulled him close and enclosed him in her arms. "Thank you, Demas. You don't know how happy I am." She let him go, turned, and ran to the man she wouldn't give up looking for.

CHAPTER 42—CLAUDE MAKES AMENDS

"Claude, if you want to see me, we have to set some rules."

"You tell me what I've got to do."

"First, you have to stop seeing that woman from the jewelry store."

"I have no problem with that."

"And you can't see anyone else while you're seeing me."

"I can live with that as well."

Adelle was now getting a head of steam. "And you've got to teach me to dance."

"You don't know how to dance?"

"Not as well as you. You must know the women stop what they're doing so they can watch you when you step out onto the floor. I need to be able to withstand their scrutiny so I don't get talked about behind my back." Adelle thought a moment. "Of course, they're going to talk about me no matter what. Just like they talk about the Creighton woman. So, I guess there's no way around it."

"We don't have to dance."

"Oh, yes, we do. You can't take that away." Adelle closed her eyes and thought about dancing with her tall, handsome man. "Tomorrow I'll see about buying a phonograph and records. We can practice here, in the front room, down the hall, in the kitchen, on the patio. Why, I'll push the furniture against the walls and we'll dance throughout the house."

"Adelle, you know what I'd like to do?"

"Name it."

"I'd like to sit in the barrel with the hot mineral water. I got so envious of Emmett the other day, I had to leave early before I made a mistake on the cabinets."

"We can do that. You'll have to wear my grandfather's bathing trunks. Is that all right? You and he have a similar build. Course, you might not like his colors. He got a little wild in his old age."

"Sure, that's fine with me."

"I'll be right back. They're in his chest."

Claude reached into a wicker basket and took out Wednesday's paper. In a loud voice he said, "Mayor Bob is supposed to light the Christmas tree in City Park at seven. Do you think we have enough time to soak and then go watch the festivities?"

Adelle came into the front room flipping the pages of a small black book. "It's from the bank—a savings account. Grandfather had another account. I think this must be where he put the money he got from selling the land to the anonymous donor." She sat in a chair. "Claude, its got a hundred thousand dollars in it."

"That's wonderful." Claude let out a low whistle. "Man, what a mountain of money. But you can't tell anyone."

"Why not?"

"People will think I was after your money all along."

"And they won't think I was after your body all along?"

"You know, Adelle, it doesn't matter what we do, we're destined to be talked about. I really feel pretty good about it. How about you?"

"Yeah, let them talk. We'll enjoy each other and walk around like we own the place. Say, you know what I'm going to do first?"

"What?"

"I'm going to make out that contract for completing the ball park. It's what grandfather wanted, and it was his money. I was selfish not to have done it already."

"And one section of bleachers is already finished. Did you find any swimming trunks?"

"No, I forgot them when I found this." Adelle turned and ran up the stairs. At the first landing she shouted over her shoulder, "There's wine in the refrigerator. If you'll open it up we can toast our good fortune in the barrel. I found you and the money, and you found me."

CHAPTER 43—THE MEN AND WOMEN SEEK AN UNDERSTANDING

Mayor Bob the Bull sat in his favorite chair and waited for Clarice to return from shopping. Her note said for him to fix supper, but he felt out of place in the kitchen. He didn't know where anything was or how to turn anything on. He wondered what he could fix. After racking his brain, he got up and went to check what items she had in the refrigerator.

Mayor Bob ended up finding a funny-looking large plate divided into sections that swiveled. From the refrigerator he took a glass jar of olives, a stick of butter, a box of crackers, and a jar of strawberry preserves. Bob looked back at the plate. "One, two, three, four, five . . . I need one more item." He scooted a few things around before he found a saucer of deviled eggs.

He filled the plate's compartments with the items from the refrigerator, found a cold beer, and set the table. He placed the swivel plate in the center and four smaller plates strategically on vacant spots around the perimeter. He then went back to his chair, drank the beer, and waited. Before long he fell asleep. He dreamed of being tied to a post and whipped. Sweat dripped from his brow. He whimpered.

Annabelle, the youngest of his two daughters, shook her father. "Wake up, Daddy. Wake up, you're having a bad dream."

Clarice stood before his chair with her arms folded. "It's about time. Where have you been?"

"Now, don't start on me, Clarice. I've had a bad day . . . and a bad night."

"Tell me about it."

The two daughters decided to listen to the excuse, so they sat on the sofa trying to blend in with the cushions. "You two young ladies carry in the groceries and put them up, then take your new clothes and hang them in the closet." The two girls didn't move. Much louder, Clarice said, "Now."

Startled, Bob jumped from his chair.

"Where do you think you're going?"

"Thought I'd help the girls bring in the groceries."

"Sit yourself down and tell me why I shouldn't kick your butt to Moccasin Gap."

"We were just going on a joy ride. Johnston . . . or, maybe it was Harold, knew of a farm for sale and we thought about buying it – as an investment. Johnston's car had a flat and his spare was flat as well. We had a cooler of beer and drank it while we pondered the situation. Then it got dark and we weren't any closer to home so we slept in the car. This morning, we got a farmer to help us repair the tire. It took all day. So here I am."

"That's not the story Johnston told Betty. Tell me about the Gilded Lilly."

Mayor Bob looked closely at his wife. "You know about that?"

"Yes, I do. Why'd you do it, Robert?"

"We were just initiating Boyd. He's never had sex. Now he probably never will. His girlfriend burnt his clothes. Anyway, someone tipped off the men from Skunk Hollow and just as soon as the girls led Boyd away, they came storming through the front door and jumped us. Fifteen minutes later, the sheriff and two deputies broke up the fight and tossed everyone in jail."

"Is that another fabrication or is it the story you're sticking with?"

"I have a couple more. One involves creatures falling from the sky, but I didn't think you'd believe it, and then there's the one where we got kidnapped by a busload of escaping women convicts, but everyone thought that was a little far-fetched."

While Clarice considered her next action, the telephone rang. She got out of her chair and walked to the telephone. A door slammed shut in a far bedroom and two white streaks shot down the hall. When Clarice was still six feet from the phone the first streak bumped into the telephone table. A hand from the second streak caught the receiver in mid-air and answered. The telephone was handed to Clarice and both streaks transformed into two pretty girls shuffling dejectedly back to their bedroom.

"Hello, Father. I'm doing fine. Yes, he made it back this afternoon. No, while I was out shopping. Yes, he's all right. A couple of scrapes on his face." Clarice started shaking her head as she listened. "Tomorrow night, Father? I don't know. Yes, well. No, it's just. All right, Father. We'll be there."

To her husband Clarice said, "Father O'Reilly wants us to be at his lecture on 'Marriage and the Family' tomorrow night."

"And, you couldn't get out of it?"

"No. You know how he can make you feel guilty when you don't agree with what he's saying."

The next evening, after a night and a day of avoiding each other's company, and right after an evening meal of three different salads and a baked squash casserole, Mayor Bob and Clarice drove to Saint Bartholomew's Holy Catholic Church. They were on time, but they were also the last couple there. As they entered the small meeting room, Edwin helped Gladys remove her coat. While he was hanging it on a round coat tree, Clarice left Mayor Bob and walked to the left side of the room where the women had congregated. Mayor Bob joined the men on the right side of the room, leaving Edwin and Gladys together in the center.

Gladys got up and walked to the refreshment table. She poured coffee from a silver carafe into a china cup on a saucer and added one cube of sugar. She brought the cup back with a small napkin and handed it to Edwin.

"Ladies and gentlemen, this is my first lecture on Marriage and the Family. I've planned two lectures this week and then a short break while I expect each of you to put into effect the principles we'll discuss. Then, we'll meet again the week before Christmas and talk about the progress we've made." Father O'Reilly looked around the room. Gladys and Edwin were holding hands.

"Summer, would you be so kind as to distribute a tablet and a pencil to each person." Father Donovan O'Reilly's eyes swept the room. "I want you to take notes." He paused. "I think we have quite a bit of work to do."

After Summer had given out the supplies, Father O'Reilly continued, "I've been wondering how to say what needed to be said.

I've talked to a few people. Even interviewed a couple who still have the romance alive. But, it wasn't enough. I've read and re-read parts of the bible: Proverbs, Ecclesiastes, Song of Solomon, the story of Ruth. I thought I was making some headway and then I listened to a woman give a speech. In just a few words, she gave my entire lecture. I tried to write it down. Please forgive me if I don't have it exactly as she so eloquently spoke.

"She said 'At all times, but especially at this time of year, we need to show steadfast faith in our God, and in our country. We need to forgive those who have offended us, to have charity in our hearts—and our pocketbooks—for those less fortunate, to have hope in the future for our children, and to have boundless love for all mankind.'"

George Satterfield raised his hand. "Father, who said that?"

"Clarice, at the Christmas tree lighting ceremony. It was her speech."

Clarice blushed. She looked at the floor.

Imogene Greenleaf said, "I think all of us women have those same sentiments in our hearts. However, it took Clarice's leadership and ability to put it into words."

"Tonight I want to break her speech into its component parts and discuss three of them. I also want to see how we can actually put them into practice. First, her second statement was 'We need to forgive those who have offended us.'

"Men, if your wives are making your life miserable, could it be retaliation for something you did to them? Women, have your husbands done something to you that you find appalling? Have they sunk below the level at which they can be forgiven? How do you determine what that level is? How can you say 'I won't have it' and then not understand how the lives of other people you love will be adversely affected? Your children, for instance.

"I know it's hard to forgive when you believe you're in the right, that your sensibilities have been stepped on, that an inconceivable injustice has been done to you. But a person in those circumstances needs to climb out of the mire of self-pity. Forgiveness is the outstanding gift you get by simply professing your Christianity, your belief in God the Creator, and in Jesus Christ, his son and our Savior and by doing a few Christian things.

"God forgives each of you. Is it inconceivable you would not also offer forgiveness to the help-mate He has given you?

"Now, the second point in her speech I want to talk about is the penultimate one. 'to have hope in the future for our children.'

"How can we have hope in the future, when we taint everything in the past that has led to the present? How can you tell your children their future is undecided because you are in a turmoil in the present over something that happened in the past?

"And the last point we'll discuss is, how do you show God you love him and all mankind, when you want to retaliate for some wrong you've suffered, to hurt the one you once held most dear—your life's companion. The person who helped you bring life and energy and meaning into your relationship. You are a team. The man, the woman, the children. These are the parts to that most magnificent of all earthly things: a living, thriving, complex, and impenetrable family. Problems should bounce off. You should be strong, undefeatable, and showing boundless love for each other.

"Can we not say enough is enough? Can we not put our differences behind us and go forth with a new beginning?

"I'm going to get something to drink while I want you to write, on one sheet of paper, what problems you have with your spouse. On another sheet write what you want the outcome to be. And on a third sheet write how you plan to take what you have and turn it into what you want.

"Remember, God is with you. He loves you. He will help you through this."

CHAPTER 44—FAYE FINDS W.W.

Faye ran to the next clearing. W.W. stood in the middle. Was it W.W.? He looked so different. He had a full beard and mustache. His hair was pulled back and tied with a dirty yellow ribbon. Faye stopped.

"W.W., do you not recognize me?"

"Ma'am, I can't remember anything prior to being pulled from the water by Chester and being cared for by Charley and Demas."

Faye walked slowly forward, she reached out and took W.W.'s hand. "Is there some place we can sit, while I tell you what I know?"

An hour later, Faye had managed to convince W.W. that he was not running from the law, that he had not done any crime, and that the reward was her idea to get the people in the area to look for a stranger. They walked to the water's edge where Demas waited with his john-boat.

Faye asked, "Is there any food left?"

"I don't know, I've been with the boat."

In just a minute or so, Demas opened the front door and held it for Faye and her future husband. Faye announced, "Everyone, this is W.W. Wainwright, my fiancé, the chief of police for Dancing Deer Arkansas, and the best friend of Trevor Radix, the Mayor of New York City."

Everyone clapped. Each knew he would've been there until something was resolved. Either Tom was the man they were looking for or he was not. Each felt good about the outcome. Each person was relieved, except Charley and Demas. The men were relieved because they would not have to go back into the woods and do combat with Demas' devices, Bear and Katy were relieved because they had unfinished business back in Dancing Deer, Horace Honeycut was relieved because he had a fantastic story for his readers, and Faye was relieved because all of her efforts were not in vain and the man of her dreams would soon be in her arms.

Katy, however was not quite so sure her unfinished business back in Dancing Deer was the business she should be about.

Horace Honeycut asked to say the blessing when everyone was finally ready to eat. He thanked the Creator for the safety provided while they hunted, for the bear remaining hibernated while Cameron lay pinned at his side, for Demas' extraordinary ability to think under pressure, for Tarleton's perception and business skill, for Chester's hospitality, and for Faye's determination. He asked for God's hand in bringing back W.W.'s memory and for everyone's safety when they returned to their homes.

At the meal, Charley had enough pewter plates and mugs but not enough silverware. The chairs from the landing dock were brought inside and two pieces of firewood not yet split were set on their ends. More silverware was brought from the barge. They made do. Charley was so proud of her ability to cook a large meal that cleaning up afterwards seemed to be no chore at all.

Chester even helped her and Demas by drying the dishes.

Honeycut said, "Miss Spencer, Tarleton sent me a telegram two days ago about the possibility of Mr. Wainwright being here. Can you make arrangements to pay him the reward?"

"Yes, I'll do that. I have the funds aboard the barge. By the way, did you know there is another five hundred offered by the railroad?"

"No, but I'll see he gets that as well." He put his hand on Tarleton's shoulder. "I'll bet the railroad will want to make a production out of it. You'll have to come into town and receive the money at a ceremony. Son, you're a rich young man. Probably have to fight off the girls."

"Shucks. It weren't nothing. Demas is the real hero. Crawling in a cave beside a hibernating bear. Now that took real courage."

Later, Horace found Katy sitting by herself and suggested she come back to West Virginia if her relationship with Bear didn't pan out. Carthage was a nice town but didn't have one attractive woman to compare with her. Katy blushed.

Tarleton counted his money three times, then handed the keys to the Dodge truck to Honeycut as the four walked back to Tarleton's house. They wondered how far along the trail they'd have to go to be past Demas' devices.

That night Tarleton asked his father if they could drive into Brewster. He wanted to buy a Christmas tree.

W.W. thanked Chester for giving him shelter, thanked Charley for saving his life, and thanked Demas for being his friend. W.W. shook Chester's hand, winked at Charley, and hugged Demas. Demas had tears in his eyes. When W.W. let Demas out of his hug he said, "Demas, you've been a special friend. I'll figure some way to finish teaching you and Charley to read and write. Don't you worry none about that. In the meantime, I've got to go find out what kind of man I was and what kind of life I lived. One of these days I'll come back."

"Here, Tom, I want you to have this." Demas held out his pocketknife.

"Demas, I can't take your knife. Besides Radix, that knife is the only thing you have."

"That's why I got to give it to you." Demas wiped his eyes and turned to look out the door.

"In that case, I'm honored to accept it."

Faye asked Jim, "How long will it take us to get back to Danville?"

"I don't rightly know. Every time we've been, we've stopped two dozen times along the way. When we do all the stopping, it's a day and a half from Chester's. So, if we crank her up to full steam and don't stop anywhere I figure about eight o'clock tonight."

"Okay, let me pay you, so when we get there all of the details will have been taken care of." She counted out three thousand dollars.

"Whew-ee, lady. I feel like a rich man."

"I think you're already a rich man. Besides having a prospering business with your brother, you're rich in friends and goodwill from the people depending on you. Jim Pike, it has been a pleasure."

Jim held out his hand. "Thank you, ma'am."

Bear rolled up his sleeping bag and placed it beside the door to the little cabin on the barge. Huddled inside around the tent heater sat the three travelers and W.W.

"Do you know any details about my life?"

Faye said, "I don't know much before you came to Dancing Deer. You've been our chief of police for four years. Before that, you were in Chicago and before that, New York City."

"Always as a policeman?"

"I think so."

"Do I have any family?"

"Yes, one sister."

"Hold on. Is her name Glenda?"

"Yes, it is. Are you starting to get your memory back?"

"I don't know. That name just popped up." W.W. crossed his leg. "Do I have any money?"

"You took out your life's savings to fund our trip to New York City. So unless the railroad has it put back for you or you left it at Glenda's, I'd say you were, more or less, broke and at my mercy."

"I need my own money."

"I have a book you helped me get published. They gave me a hefty advance royalty. Most of it is in the bank in Dancing Deer. When we get married, that money will be yours."

"But I need my own money."

"How about we write another book? This time about your adventure in West 'By God' Virginia. Maxine will publish it without any quibble. Half of the royalty will be yours and you can spend it any way you like."

"Good. I have to figure a way to repay Chester and his family."

"How about I loan you some of the money now? You can pay me back when we split the advance on the new book."

CHAPTER 45—W.W. PAYS FOR HIS KEEP

The hotel in downtown Danville was almost deserted. A desk clerk slept in a chair behind the counter and the lights in the dining room were turned off. Bear walked up to the counter and rang the bell. The startled desk clerk dropped the book he had laying on his stomach and jumped up like a sentry caught asleep at his post. After realizing where he was, and what he'd been doing, the desk clerk walked to the counter rubbing the sleep from the corners of his eyes.

"Yes, sir?"

"Have you got any rooms?"

"Yeah, most are empty. Some hotels fill up for the holidays, we go the other route."

"Okay, we need four singles."

"No problem." He handed out four slips of paper. "I need a name for each room."

Faye set her one piece of luggage down and pulled her pocketbook from her purse. "Bear, I'd like adjoining rooms for me and W.W."

"You're not going to scare him back to the wildwood are you?"

"No, but I'd like to be handy if he wants to talk."

"He sure has been quiet. I think he feels like the little kid going to camp for the first time with people he doesn't know."

Katy put her hand through Bear's arm. "He reminds me of a puppy just taken away from his mother. Look at him sitting by the fire. Have you ever seen a more pitiful sight?"

Faye gave her purse to Katy. "Here, pay for the rooms." She walked to W.W. and sat on the rock ledge in front of the fireplace. "What's the matter, honey?"

"I don't know. I'm wondering if I'll be able to help or if I'll be a hindrance. I don't know how I can adjust. I had life with Chester and his two kids figured out, but now I've got to start over and I feel lost."

199

"Honey, you leave everything to me. Whatever you need, I'll get it for you. I'll be at your side every step of the way. I have plenty of money for both of us. You don't have to work. You don't have to do anything."

"No, you don't understand. I don't want to be taken care of. I want to work. I just don't know what I can do. I don't know how I'll fit in."

Bear and Katy walked from the desk clerk's counter holding out two keys. "Let's get the luggage to the rooms and see if we can find a restaurant open for supper."

The desk clerk directed them to a local diner. A few people were sitting in closely spaced booths.

Katy said, "Let's sit at the counter. There on the end where it curves." On the way she whispered to her younger sister, "Bear wouldn't be able to sit at any of those tiny booths."

"Oh, that's right." Then at a higher volume Faye said, "W.W., you sit in the middle."

The waitress brought glasses of water, napkins, and flatware. "Here are the menus. Do you want breakfast or dinner?"

Bear said, "Depends. Let us look at the menu first."

After the waitress left, each person looked at a single page with dinner items on one side and breakfast items on the flipside. In a minute, everyone but W.W. had decided. W.W. had his eyes squinted and had been holding the menu at different distances.

"You used to wear glasses. You probably lost them when you fell into the water. Do you remember holding close a little girl?"

"No."

"She was rescued. Not one broken bone. Her mother told me to write if I was able to find you." Faye took W.W.'s menu. "They have a pot roast with boiled potatoes and onions. There's meatloaf. Or how about fried chicken?"

"The chicken sounds good. I want a salad too."

"Tomorrow, we'll see about getting you another pair of glasses."

That night when they returned, W.W. ran a tub of hot water. While it filled, he walked to Bear's room and knocked. After his second series of knocks Bear opened Katy's door and stuck out his head.

"Do you have a razor I could borrow?"

"Man, you'll need scissors first. If I were you, I'd wash it tonight and tomorrow we'll both get haircuts and a shave. I do have a razor, and you're welcome to it, but without the scissors I don't think it'll do much good."

W.W. lathered up a bar of Castile Soap and saturated his hair with soap and water. After the second effort, he thought it felt clean to the touch and went to work on other parts of his body. Fifteen minutes later, he let the water out and refilled the tub. This time he luxuriated in the hot water. There was a knock on his bathroom door.

"Can I scrub your back?"

"Uh . . . with what?"

"If there's no brush, I could use a washcloth or my fingernails."

"Ma'am, I don't have any clothes on."

"Neither do I."

The next day Faye and Katy deposited the two men at a barbershop while they looked for transportation to Carthage.

"So, Bear, what can you tell me about Dancing Deer?"

"Not much to tell, really. It's a pretty little town about twice the size of Danville. I think it's got six . . . maybe, eight thousand people. The train hasn't made it there yet. They say the terrain is too mountainous for it to be profitable. I guess they mean that it would cost too much to lay the tracks for the small number of people and tonnage of goods it would haul.

"We got a real nice Main Street. The families of the city council have been on a tear painting the retail stores. There's a rumor going around that Bill Potter made them do it. Oh, I bet you don't remember Bill. He's the town nasty. But lately, he's turned a corner and shown everyone he has a nice side after all. Most people are withholding judgment, thinking he'll be back to his old ornery self before long."

"We got a nice newspaper and a damn good baseball team. They were building a new ball park, but that's now on hold. We got City Park. It'll rival any park anywhere. It's got a thermal spring for year-round bathing, lighted pathways that wind around flower beds and a rocky stream, and piped-in music. There's kids everywhere—playing marbles and hopscotch and skipping rope—and a church on most every corner."

"Sounds like a wonderful place to live."

"We think so."

The barber leaned over. "Do they need a barbershop?"

"Probably. You'd have to learn to whistle a tune while you worked though."

That afternoon, Horace Honeycut pulled up in his Dodge truck. "Anybody need a lift to the thriving metropolis of Carthage?"

The four travelers had just come out of a dry goods store where Faye had purchased W.W. two new shirts, two pairs of corduroy pants, and assorted other items including a brown pair of Red Wing shoes.

"Mr. Honeycut, you're just in the nick of time." Faye slung her sack into the bed of the truck. "We got to go to the Sundown Hotel first. The desk clerk's holding our luggage behind the counter."

Bear and W.W. got into the bed while the two ladies crowded into the cab with Horace. Katy sat in the middle astraddle the gear shifter sticking up from the floor. Her leg resting against Honeycut's.

To W.W., Bear said, "You should've gotten that coat."

"Naw, I'll be all right. It didn't fit."

The next day, Faye and Katy got up early and had Honeycut drive them to the train station, so they could find out about the next train heading west. They got back to the hotel in time to eat breakfast with the men.

"Faye, I can't leave before I take care of some loose ends."

"Okay, the tickets weren't for assigned seating. We can use them anytime. What kind of loose ends are you talking about?"

"I need to find out if Demas and Charley can enroll in the school in Brewster."

"I can help you there. My brother-in-law is on their school board," said Horace. "After we eat I'll drive you over."

"Mr. Honeycut, are there any places that sell boats and motors?"

"Yeah, sure, we're on the river. They got motorboats at the marina and we got a Scott Atwater and an Evinrude dealership in town."

Lost in Appalachia / Lambert

"How about a sporting goods store and a large mercantile."

"No problem."

At the school in Brewster, it was decided that a special tutor would get Demas and Charley up to speed, and then they'd start attending classes with students their own age. They were given some simple readers and papers for Chester to sign. On the way out the door, W.W. said. "You might not have noticed, but neither of the children have shoes . . . or decent clothes. Faye, could I borrow some money, so Mr. Honeycut can see to it they have proper clothes. Demas once told me the kids made fun of him because he couldn't read or write and he didn't have shoes."

"Don't worry about it. It will be my pleasure to furnish them whatever they need in that department."

"Okay, let's go to the marina to see how we might furnish the means to get them to school. Faye, you got enough money to buy a motorboat?"

Horace said, "Before I forget, I'd like an address. I'll send everyone copies of my paper when I run the story."

"That will be fantastic. Do you have plenty of pictures?"

"Yeah, one of John hanging upside-down sixty feet up in a tree, another of W.W. laughing at us in the distance, and still another of all of us eating Thanksgiving dinner."

"What about the Pike Brothers' Floating Store? You can also have the negative we used for the poster." Faye smiled at the newspaper editor. "That's the makings of a great story. And tomorrow, I think W.W. will be adding a nice farewell." She turned to W.W. "I still have three thousand in cash and a letter from our bank. They'll just have to make a telephone call."

It took all day for the visit to Brewster and for W.W.'s purchases. That night he and Faye had dinner alone as Bear and Katy took in a flick.

"Faye, tell me about us."

"W.W., you might not think you are right now, but I can tell you that you are the most wonderful person to be around. You know tidbits of information on almost any subject a person can dream up. You're not a real good dancer, but you try your best instead of sitting on the sidelines with a bucket of excuses. You treat me well. You pull out my chair, make sure that I'm comfortable, that all my needs are cared for. That's why I hover around you. I'm trying to do for you what you'd be doing for me. I love you."

"Have I ever been married? Do I have any children?"

"Not to my knowledge. You told me your police work was your life. There wasn't much time for anything else. No, that's not exactly right. You had a girlfriend for four years. She was a prostitute and you spent every Wednesday night with her. She was murdered and you helped to solve the case. That's what my book is about."

"Do you have a copy with you?"

"I always have a . . . Oh, W.W., we forgot to get your glasses. We'll take care of that Monday morning after we get back from taking that new boat to Chester's. You can read my book on the train ride to Arkansas. In Little Rock we'll catch a bus for the last leg."

"I don't remember how to be a policeman."

"That's okay, because you won't have time anyway. We got to start on the book while everything's still fresh in your memory." Faye took a big sip of iced tea. "W.W., there's something I've got to tell you." She picked up her napkin and twisted it in her hands. She then sit up straight and looked down at her dinner.

"What is it?"

Tears were streaming down her cheek. "W.W., I can't . . . I can't . . ."

"You can't what?"

"I can't cook."

"Good Lord, woman, don't scare me like that. I thought you were going to say you couldn't marry me. That you were already married."

"I can't cook a lick. My mother and I made cookies. That's it. W.W., can you live on oatmeal and raisin cookies?"

"No, but I can live on love—and I can learn to cook."

"I think I can learn, if you'll give me some time—and a little leeway?"

"Doll, you can have all the time and leeway you need."

"Oh, W.W, that's what you always called me."

"What?"

"Doll." Faye jumped up from her seat and went around the table. She kissed W.W. on the mouth. "It's coming back, W.W. It's slow—a word here, a word there—but it's coming back." Faye looked around the restaurant. Several people looked her way. She blushed and sat down. "W.W., do you feel like dessert?"

CHAPTER 46—FAREWELL, APPALACHIA

Bear looked at the loaded boat and told Katy they would do well to go shopping. So when W.W. and Faye started the outboard motor and headed downstream, Bear and Katy headed to the main shopping area hand in hand.

Bear said, "I need to buy some souvenirs and some Christmas presents for my family."

"How many are there in your family?"

"Four. Besides my parents, I have a brother and a sister. Sampson, my brother, was the one who gave you instructions on playing pool."

"No one's ever given me instructions on playing pool."

"Are you sure? Sampson's almost as big as me, just a little shorter."

"Bear, I've been to your pool hall twice. The first time the guy behind the bar said you were in training and living at the Ritz. The second time was when I talked to you about coming here with me."

"You didn't come to Snockered and talk to Sampson? You didn't go to the jukebox while several of the men raced to put in their money for you?"

"No, it wasn't me."

"I'll bet that Sampson has a girlfriend and doesn't know it."

"Or, you do."

"I have one, and I know it."

When W.W. pulled the new lacquered-wood motorboat with the painted red stripes and powerful Evinrude motor to the dock, Demas, Chester, and Charley came running out of their cabin.

"Santa Claus was in Carthage. He asked if I could deliver some presents to a special family he'd been neglecting."

"What ya got, Tom—I mean W.W."

"Well, let's see, Demas. Help me get the boat tied up snug so I can stand up without falling overboard."

"She sure is a pretty boat, Tom."

"This long leather scabbard is for Chester." W.W. held it out. "I believe this sack with the fabric hanging out is for Charley. There's several bolts of fabric, and thread, and buttons, and zippers, and lace and patterns. And several pair of scissors—all different sizes. You've also got that big box in the middle."

"For me? They're all for me?"

"Yep, and in this sack are toys. There's puzzles, checkers, Chinese checkers, yo-yos, paddle balls, horseshoes, and a football."

"Are they mine?"

"They're for everyone, Demas."

Chester said, "Tom, I don't know what to say. I ain't never fired a gun like this before. It's got a scope and everything."

"You also got a shotgun somewhere at the bottom of the sacks. And several boxes of ammunition. Charley, do you know what that is?"

"Yes, sir. It's a treadle sewing machine."

"And here's a sack for Radix. I got him a new collar and some puppy toys."

"Also, you each have a hundred dollar credit at the Crown Mercantile in Brewster. Use it for anything."

"Tom, did you get anything for me?"

"Demas? Faye, we forgot to get Demas something."

"That's okay." Demas shuffled his feet. "I'm just glad everything worked out good for you, Tom."

"Demas, the boat is yours."

"The boat? Mine? Holy, mackerel."

"You get that from one of the books?"

"Yep."

"You got to be sixteen to drive a car, but there's no age requirement to drive a boat. I figure you'll be a fast study. The way you handle your dad's boat, this one will be a piece of cake. You also have five-hundred dollars credit at the Brewster Marina. You can use it for gasoline or accessories. You might want to get a knob for the steering wheel. I figured you'd need some means of transportation to get to school. They're expecting you and Charley in Brewster on Tuesday.

"Tomorrow Mr. Honeycut will meet us at the Carthage Marina dock. Faye and I have to catch the train to Arkansas after I get a pair of glasses, but Mr. Honeycut will take you and Charley to get shoes and clothes to wear to school."

"Chester, I have papers for you to sign so they can enroll. I think Demas and Charley also got an appointment at the doctor's office for a shot or two. The school requires it."

"Tom, This is wonderful. We ain't had Christmas since Molly died."

Demas hugged W.W., then helped Charley get the sewing machine on the make-shift dock. W.W. handed Chester and Faye the packages from the boat and then handed Demas the boat's ignition keys.

Chester said, "I'm glad you and your lady friend are staying the night. Bright and early tomorrow morning, we'll have Demas try his hand at the new boat. I'd like to go with him until he gets a few miles under his belt."

"I think that would be great, Chester."

"If you haven't eaten yet, Charley fixed cornpone pie for supper."

THE END

Author Bio

Ron Lambert, an examined life

As an accountant in a small West Texas town, I spend my days studying the bank statements and tax returns of other people's businesses. I classify, summarize, and display their financial transactions in some meaningful format. I love creating order out of chaos.

I'm middle-aged and twice married—with the second blessed from heaven. Four grown children, their children, two bobbing tails of barking energy, and one sly cat round out my cache of treasure.

Over the years I have owned and operated two boutique retail stores, several service businesses, one ranch, and one restaurant. I have been prosperous and poor, with wild fluctuations in between. At present, being neither rich nor poor, I consider my status as deeply entrenched in middle class—a term bandied about by politicians and economists.

A few years ago, in an effort to restore my youth, I purchased an old sofa on two wheels. Since that initial existential groping, I have occasionally strapped sacks of clothes, maps, and a compass that doesn't seem to work onto the back cushion. After kissing my wife, I set out for adventure and story and to find answers to the big questions. Usually, after only a week or so, I realize what I left behind was more important than what I set out to find and drive a day and a night hell-bent-for-leather back home.

I then settle into an old and comfortable routine. I read a few books, attend a few plays, daydream of new horizons, and plan my next adventure. I kept a journal on my first excursion. It was such an exhilarating experience: rewriting the journal and incorporating the pictures I took that I became intoxicated to the point I wrote a novel.

At present, with pen on fire, I am writing my eighth book. I'll win prestigious awards and be asked to speak at the local library if someone would read what I have written.

If you're looking for an evening spent with colorful and mesmerizing characters, if you want to immerse yourself in a rollicking good story, enthrall yourself to the point of madness, go two days without bathing, then have I got a story for you.

Additional Novels
The Dancing Deer Story

Soon all will be available in multiple formats at Amazon.com and www.printersguildpublishing.com Trade Paperbacks in perfect binding can be purchased at our corporate office and from display stands in several of our fine businesses in Columbus, Texas

Dancing Deer (Book 1)

Dancing Deer is the embodiment of small-town America. When asked, she sent her sons to war. This is the story of The Calhoun—one of those boys. It's also about his fellow combatants, the men he served, the men he fought, and the women he loved.

There is the French Resistance, the German Gestapo, *Midge at the Mike*, Anzio Annie, the *Gustav Line*, and the US Army's Forty-Fifth Infantry campaigning from Sicily through Italy, France, and Germany to push back the formidable Germans. But this story is so much more.

Find a comfortable chair and settle in with a great new book. You won't be disappointed.

The Last Dance (Book 2)

Bill Potter is charged with murdering his Friday night squeeze. His bumbling lawyer steps out of a dead-end job of contracts and leases to save Bill from being strapped to "Old Spanky." Bill's wife returns after a twenty year absence to muddy the waters and it's up to her and Pepe, the womanizing Resistance fighter and WWI spy from France, to solve the case.

The Measure of a Man (Book 3)

A group of Cuban immigrants decide to barnstorm the Midwest by entertaining the towns they come to with a game of ball. When they get to Dancing Deer the men on the city council con Bill Potter into a wager for more than they can afford to lose. Bill's position is that the Men from Dancing Deer will prevail. With a team of misfits and one win under their belts, Bill goes searching for a new manager. His ex-wife is traveling throughout the Western US with Pepe, the French womanizer. She knows more about ball than anyone and he has to convince her to come back and once again save him from the wolves at the door.

Lost in Appalachia (Book 4)

Dancing Deer's Chief of Police is lost in the mountains of West Virginia. Suffering from an injury, he can't remember who he is or why he's lost. Two kids take him in and hide him from a determined fiancée. The chief of police is in the process of teaching the kids how to read when the fiancée posts a big reward for knowledge of his whereabouts. The chief thinks he must have committed a major crime for someone to pony up such a large bounty. With the children hiding him, the chief has to decide what to do when he learns the shady secrets of an earlier life.

Christmas in Dancing Deer (Book 5)

St. Bartholomew's is consolidating its orphanage, but the children don't want to be separated. They come up with an alternative plan to present to the church, but the women of Dancing Deer bring the orphan girls into their homes for the holidays. The orphan boys leave on their own in the snow three days before Christmas and spend a night with a burdened bank robber in a desolated cabin. This is a classic tale of how good triumphs over evil in an adult sitting.

Beggarman, Thief (Book 6)

A story of a bank robber who finds his moment of epiphany in a shack with six lost little boys. He goes home after twenty years on the lamb to have Christmas with his family and to right his wrongs. But he finds his past is in hot pursuit and the new life he has found is in jeopardy. He runs away in the clutches of a pretty lady evangelist who is taking her show on the road to the very town where he committed his last crime. A story that can be enjoyed by everyone.

Toe to Toe with A Drunken Philosopher

This is really one story in three parts. First we have the high school philosophy teacher who has to resign his position much as Aristotle had to when the authorities in Athens came looking for him.

Part number two is of an indigent Irish family who emigrate from the Emerald Isle. The little Irish boy in the family grows up to become a priest.

Then the third part pits the philosopher and the priest in a contest of wits.

Racing the Wind (Book 7 in the series, but not yet finished)

The story of a boy with plans to someday build bridges or design skyscrapers. He decides to start with a racer in the All American Soapbox Derby. Problems, orchestrated by his main adversary, creep into the racer's production. The boy has to rely on the help of a fellow classmate—a girl—to find the source of his problems and to finish the racer and the race.

Order Form

Book Name	Qty	Price	Extension
Dancing Deer	☐	$17.95	_____
The Last Dance	☐	$15.95	_____
The Measure of a Man	☐	$15.95	_____
Lost in Appalachia	☐	$15.95	_____
Christmas in Dancing Deer	☐	$15.95	_____
Beggarman, Thief	☐	$15.95	_____
Toe to Toe with a Drunken Philosopher	☐	$15.95	_____
Racing the Wind	☐	$15.95	_____

Sub-Total _____

Sales Tax (for Texas purchases) @8.25% _____

Shipping: $4.00 for 1st Book
$2.00 for each Additional _____

Grand Total _____

Would you like your book(s) autographed? Yes ☐ No ☐

Would you like your book(s) wrapped? Yes ☐ No ☐

To_____ From_____

Order Form (continued)

Name _____

Shipping Address:

    Military APO   _____

    Street or PO Box   _____

    State and Zip   _____

Telephone _____

Payment:

    Check Enclosed   ☐

    Credit Card:

        Discover   ☐

        Visa   ☐

        MasterCard   ☐

Card Number   _____

Expiration Date   _____

Code (on back)   _____

Keep Credit Card Information for future purchases   ☐

Order Form (instructions)

Boxes   Place quantity or checkmark (X) where applicable

Mail Completed Form To:
>   Printers Guild Publishing House, llc
>   425 Spring Street, Suite 101
>   Columbus, Texas 78934-2461

Or Fax Form to:
>   (979) 733-0015

Or Call-In Your Order during business hours:
>   (979) 732-2962

For Pick-Up:
>   You are welcome to come by our office in the Stafford Opera House at 425 Spring Street, Suite 101, Columbus, Texas to pick up your order and save shipping costs or to talk with the author.

Please call (979) 732-2962 to make sure someone will be there.

Security
>   We do not share any of your information with anyone. We do not keep your credit card information unless you check the box allowing us to do so for future purchases.

www.ingramcontent.com/pod-product-compliance
Lightning Source LLC
Chambersburg PA
CBHW050524260626
47157CB00004B/1464